AMISH
ADVENTURE

AMISH
ADVENTURE

Barbara Smucker

HERALD PRESS
Scottdale, Pennsylvania

Acknowledgements

I would like to express special gratitude for interviews and friendly visits with various Old Order Amish and Old Order Mennonite families; to Orland Gingerich, David Yantzi, Amsey Weber, Roy Brubacher, and Ian Walker of Ontario; and to Winfield Fretz of Kansas and Laura Kogel-Smucker of New York City.

All the characters in this book are fictitious, as is the village of Milltown. Ontario.

Dedicated to the memory of
Christian Schmucker I,
a devout Amishman
who migrated from Montbeliard, France
to Reading, Pennsylvania
in 1752
seeking religious freedom.
He was the great-great-great-great-grandfather
of my husband, Donovan.
His many children subsequently settled
in Pennsylvania, Ohio and Ontario.

1

Ian McDonald struggled with the heavy swinging doors of the Chicago highrise where he lived with his father. A swirling late-summer wind off Lake Michigan was blowing his tousled hair into red strands over his eyes, one of his shoelaces was untied and tripping him up, and the book bag on his back was unzipped and things were spilling out of it. Several people pushed past him. Not one of them offered to help.

Ian reluctantly put down the heavy wooden box he was carrying. It contained the most exciting gift he had ever received. It had not been easy to carry it onto the North Avenue bus and then walk five blocks down busy Division Street to his building.

Only an hour ago, at the end of the summer-school day, just as he was leaving his grade seven science class, his teacher Mr. Riddle had walked up to him:

"Ian, I know how much you like animals. I guess cats and dogs aren't allowed in your apartment building, but I see no reason why you can't have the white rat from the laboratory until the Fall term. He's tame, and doesn't eat much. You could keep him in this box until you get a cage. He can even run loose around the apartment when you're at home."

The white rat! Ian was surprised. He desperately wanted a pet at home. But he and Dad were moving in three weeks. That's why he was taking summer-school courses. He tried to explain the problem.

"Well, bring him back to me whenever you have to," Mr. Riddle said. He let Ian hold the long, smooth animal with its trembling pink tail while he filled a large wooden box with chopped paper and grains of rat food, then slid a jar of the special food into Ian's book bag.

Ian couldn't say no. Instead he burst out excitedly, "Thank you. I'll take very good care of him," and walked with springing steps into the windy summer day. All the way home he had been careful to keep the box upright. A chill had run down his back at the thought of losing his new pet.

Now, at the apartments, he finally managed to jam one of the glass doors open and force his way in. He glared at the apartment security guard in his flashing red uniform. The man just stood there like a wound-up tin soldier.

When Ian got inside the passenger elevator, two smartly dressed residents edged away from him as if they thought the box might be holding a bomb. Ian was going to tell them that it was only a rat, but decided not to bother. Someone pressed the number of his floor — 17.

It was hard to get out of the elevator when it stopped because a heavy-set woman was stepping on his shoelace. He jerked his foot sharply away.

·"Stop that!" the woman shouted. She reminded Ian of his Aunt Clem who lived in Toronto.

He walked carefully down the carpeted hall of the seventeenth floor to his apartment door and rang the bell for Mrs. Coutts, the new temporary housekeeper.

"I think you'll like her," his father had said when she arrived the week before last. "She's Scottish and I suspect she's also a pretty good cook."

She didn't answer Ian's ringing, so he put the box down, got his own key and opened the door himself. Mrs. Coutts didn't hear him enter. She was in the kitchen, chattering loudly to a friend on the telephone.

8

"The boy is the spitting image of his father," she said, laughing. "He's tall and skinny, with a mop of red hair." She paused for a second. Ian coughed, but she paid no attention and rattled on with her report.

"No, I wouldn't say handsome.... Their faces are too rugged and covered with pale freckles." She laughed again. Ian felt like throwing something at her.

"They're pretty stubborn too. Red hair goes with hot tempers, you know.... Sometimes you'd think there were two rockets living in the house, exploding one minute, then going out the next...."

Ian started to sneak towards his bedroom, but he slipped on the freshly waxed floor in the hallway. His book bag crashed into the hall lamp, but the box was safe. It landed upright on the thick entrance rug.

"Gracious!" Mrs. Coutts cried, racing from the phone.

Ian's face flushed with anger and embarrassment. He didn't mind too much what Mrs. Coutts had said. He liked to be compared to his Dad. But she exaggerated. He and his father didn't explode all the time. They argued and they disagreed, but they liked to be together. After dinner tonight they were going to finish reading *Frozen Fire,* a dramatic story about the Arctic. Dad was an engineer for a major oil company and his next job was going to be near the North Pole; in three weeks they were moving from Chicago to Inuvik in the Northwest Territories. Ian could hardly wait. He thought about it day and night.

"Such a mess, Ian" Mrs. Coutts lamented, viewing the disarray in the hall. "And I just tidied everything."

"Wait until you see what I've got in the box." Ian refused to allow her fussiness to dampen his excitement. He cautiously opened the lid.

"It's a live animal!" Mrs. Coutts cried, looking inside.

"Of course it is," Ian laughed. "It's a white rat."

"A rat!" Mrs. Coutts shrieked. She ran for the bathroom and slammed the door. Ian could hear her sliding the bolt into the lock.

"Ian." Mrs. Coutts' voice came through the door, shrill and squeaky as if a bone was caught in her throat. "Take that rat out of the apartment at once. If you don't, I'll call the manager and tell him to send the exterminator."

9

The rat cowered in the corner of the box and shivered. Ian rubbed the animal's back gently with his thumb.

"I'm going to call you Angel," he murmured softly. "You're so white." Then he raised his voice in the direction of the bathroom door.

"Stop yelling, Mrs. Coutts. You're scaring Angel."

"Angel?" Mrs. Coutts opened the door slightly. Her wispy gray hair had tumbled down, making a web over her eyes, and some bright red lipstick appeared to streak down her chin.

"I will not stay in this apartment another minute with a rat, Ian." Mrs. Coutts was hysterical. "I'm going to call your father's emergency number at the oil company."

Ian couldn't believe what he was hearing.

"You're acting as if I'd brought a polar bear in here." He was rapidly losing respect for this new housekeeper. He closed the lid of the wooden box and picked it up carefully.

"I'm taking Angel downstairs to Tony's apartment," he said angrily. "I won't be back until you've left and Dad is home."

Then he walked out, banging the apartment door shut with his foot.

2

Ian hurried to the service elevator which was often filled with furniture being moved in and out of the building. It was empty. He placed the rat box beside him and punched the button for Basement.

His one good friend Tony lived at the bottom of the twenty-five storeys of Tower B. Tony will like Angel, Ian thought grimly, seething inside at Mrs. Coutts' hysterics.

Tony Taboli was almost the opposite of Ian — chubby and dark-haired, with shining eyes. Ian had found him one day when he had punched the wrong button of the service elevator and slid to the bottom of the building. The door had opened in front of the Tabolis' basement apartment. Tony's father, in his underwear top, tended the giant furnaces of Tower B. His plump mother cooked and cleaned and cared for Tony and his

10

three small sisters. The parents mainly spoke Italian, but always welcomed Ian with smiles. That first day Tony had invited Ian to play marbles on the cement space out of doors between the two tall apartment buildings.

"One day the buildings will breathe and squeeze the air out of us and smash the marbles," Tony had predicted with delicious horror. But they kept on playing there anyway.

The two boys didn't go to the same school and they also went to different churches — Tony was a Catholic and Ian sometimes attended Fourth Presbyterian with his father — but they had got used to meeting in the hours before dinner.

This afternoon Tony happened to be standing in front of the elevator as the door rolled open. He saw the rat box at once and helped Ian lift it.

"It's a tame white rat." Ian's excitement was returning. "Mr. Riddle at school gave him to me."

"Oh!" Tony said with some unease. He looked cautiously over his shoulder.

"Let's take him outside between the buildings, Ian. Poppa fights the big, brown rats down here. He's always shouting 'They are the enemy of the people!' " Tony shook his fists.

They carried Angel to the sliver of fresh air and thin blue sky between the buildings that was their hide-out. An hour went by as they greeted the strange new creature, feeling his sniffing on their fingertips, discovering the warmth of his white fur. They made a plan to build a cage for him in the secret place to protect him from Mrs. Coutts.

Then Ian checked his watch. Mrs. Coutts would have gone now, and it was time for his father to be home. Tony lifted the box into the elevator.

Upstairs, on floor 17, Ian's apartment door was ajar. Was his Dad impatient for him to arrive? He stepped inside, holding the box. His father was there, pacing back and forth across the living-room rug. His tie was loose and his thick red hair stood up in rumpled peaks.

What had Mrs. Coutts said to him? Could a white rat cause all this pacing and worry?

Ian opened the box in front of him.

"Look, Dad."

"It's a nice pet, Ian," was all his father said, and continued his walking.

11

"What's wrong, Dad?" Ian was apprehensive.

Andrew McDonald slumped into a chair, his long legs jutting up into awkward angles in front of him. There was trouble and anxiety in his look.

"Ian, we always talk things over, don't we?" His father looked directly at him.

Ian readily agreed. Dad's job as an engineer and trouble-shooter for the oil company had taken them from country to country together. They had laughed often about the apartment building they had rented one year in Amsterdam. It had hung over the side of a wide canal and all their furniture had to be hoisted through the enormous front window from a barge below. In school there Ian had learned more Dutch than Dad, and on weekends they had bicycled through the country on special paths, stopping for hearty lunches at the cheese markets. One year he and his Dad had lived in Calgary with its blue mountains and white patches of snow in the distance. He had learned to play ice hockey there.

They had shared Dad's passionate concern about the environment, too.

"People are sucking the oil and the minerals from the earth as if they'll be there for ever, Ian," his father had often said. They had tested water from Lake Michigan for poisons and pollution. They had petitioned the people in their apartment to use less electricity.

Their skipping from country to country had been exciting, but it upset their only close relative, Aunt Clem, who felt roots should be in one place, permanent and deep.

Ian's father still sat morosely in his chair and looked at his son.

"I've got bad news, Ian." Dad's long, slim fingers tangled through his hair. "There's no way to make it pleasant, so I'd better just tell you."

Ian was really alarmed now. He closed the lid of the rat box. Angel didn't seem important any more.

"You know the job in the Northwest Territories starts in three weeks." Andrew McDonald spoke slowly, watching Ian. "Well, I've just found out much of my work for the first six months will be on off-shore oil rigs in the Beaufort Sea."

Ian listened closely. His father's eyes moved out of habit to the picture on the mantelpiece of a pretty young girl with laughing eyes and curling black hair. She was Ian's mother, but he had never known her. She had died the day he was born.

"It's like this." Andrew McDonald had stopped his postponing. "The company says you can't come along this time. There's no place for a boy on an oil rig.... I asked about a different assignment up there, Ian, but the answer was no. Keeping my job depends on going without you."

This was a hit in the stomach. Ian felt breathless and sick at the same time.

"But where will I go? I can't live here alone with Mrs. Coutts. You can't just leave me, Dad."

Two big hands clamped over Ian's shoulders. "Let's work this out together, Ian. You know I wouldn't leave you on your own." He paused. "I called Aunt Clem in Toronto this afternoon. She'd be happy to have you live with her for six months. She has a large house and there's a school only eight blocks away."

"Aunt Clem!" Ian exploded. Anger surfaced to cover up his hurt. An elongated picture loomed before him of stocky, domineering Aunt Clem with her sweeping gray hair and her dreary house filled with antique furniture.

Ian bent down abruptly and lifted the lid of Angel's box. He picked up the sleek white rat and held him close.

Andrew McDonald walked to the picture on the mantelpiece and stood in front of it. Ian followed him.

"You told me we would always stay together."

"Ian." His father was stern. "Life is filled with many disappointments. They have to be faced and made the best of. Shouting and begging won't help."

Ian listened. His father always plunged into problems with no excuses and no easy escapes. But how could he bury this disappointment? Living near the North Pole with Dad had been his dream for months.

13

3

Huge, empty packing boxes crouched around Ian, looking like faceless intruders. Tomorrow they would be filled with household goods and stacked in some dark, airless warehouse. Then the apartment where they had lived for over a year would be deserted.

Ian stared out of the seventeenth-floor window at the treeless sky. The red autumn sun, far below, was sinking behind a row of toylike blocks of buildings. A fat pigeon that always came for seed which Ian scattered on the outside grilled-in porch pecked unknowingly at his last meal there. After purchasing a securely locked cage to pacify Mrs. Coutts, Ian had finally had to return Angel to Mr. Riddle.

A well of misery had been simmering inside Ian for the last three weeks. He tried to hide it, like clamping a lid over his heart, but today it seemed to rise into a steam of anger and despair. It had to spill out somewhere. He searched for his father and found him bent in his usual lean, angular way over his desk of littered books and papers.

Ian stood in front of him, miserable and defiant.

"I won't go!" he shouted abruptly. He had been trying for the past three weeks to be understanding of his father's job. "I won't live with Aunt Clem in that creepy old house in Toronto. I don't care if she's our only close relative. You promised I could go with you. I've always gone with you."

Ian's father looked up, red-eyed and weary.

"What's happened to you, Ian?" he sighed. "I thought we settled this whole problem three weeks ago. You don't think I want to be separated from you either, do you? I wanted us to share this experience."

Andrew McDonald rubbed his eyes. Then he relaxed into the banter and kidding that usually ended with both of them laughing.

"Come on, Ian. Red-haired Scotsmen have to keep their tempers from boiling up or else they sound like a flock of screeching bluejays."

14

It didn't work. Ian was too upset.

"What was the point of spending all those nights looking at maps and reading *Frozen Fire* and *People of the Deer*," he stormed. "You said it would be the experience of a lifetime to live in the North. We were going to meet some of the Inuit and see the midnight sun. Now you're going without me. It isn't fair."

"Ian." His father was cross. "I've had to say this far too often. The company has an emergency and they need me at once. I also have my own urgent concerns about the environment up there. They won't let you come with me, and that's final. I'm sorry, but it's either Aunt Clem's house or a boarding school."

Ian groaned remembering the many new schools he had attended because of Dad's travelling job. It wasn't easy to make new friends in them. Lately he'd been getting bad grades and his Chicago school in the winter had crowded classes, but at least he could look forward to evenings with Dad. Who would he read aloud with at Aunt Clem's? Who would play chess with him before bedtime? Where was he going to find another friend like Tony?

If Mrs. Coutts had walked into the dishevelled apartment at this moment she would probably have made some tart comment about red hair, Scottish background, quick tempers and stubborn wills.

Most of Ian's McDonald ancestors had left their native Highlands in Scotland to migrate to the forests of Ontario and the untamed banks of Lake Erie. They were determined frugal, honest and hard-working people. They cleared the forests and built farm homes to last for ever. But Andrew McDonald had left the farm before he went to university to become an engineer. He had not gone back. In fact he never talked about his rural youth.

Ian continued to stand obstinately before his father.

"All right," he said, trying to soften the attack. "I'm glad you work for the oil company. I'm glad you try to save the environment. But I still want to go with you."

Andrew McDonald looked with concern at his tall, thin twelve-year old son.

He sat with Ian on top of one of the packing boxes and

placed a strong arm around his shoulders. "Look, it'll only be for six months," he said.

Ian's head began to ache and a great lump filled his throat. He hid both of them with muffled comments.

"I won't have any friends in the new school. Even Aunt Clem is like a stranger. And all those antiques in her house make the place seem haunted."

"Nonsense." Andrew McDonald smiled. "I know Clem isn't the easiest person to live with. She's strong-willed and outspoken. But her house is solid and warm and it isn't haunted. You might even get to like it."

Ian didn't answer.

"You'll be good for her, Ian. She's been a lonely widow since Uncle Malcolm was killed in World War Two."

"Dad!" Ian interrupted. "That was years and years ago." But he felt defeated. He couldn't even go and talk with Tony. The Tabolis were in Italy on holiday and he and Tony had said goodbye last week.

"Now, no more arguments, Ian." His father held him close for a brief moment. "I worry about you a great deal. Now off to bed at once. I'll see you first thing in the morning. Jack Turner from the company is coming at seven o'clock to drive you to Toronto."

Ian started down the hall to his bedroom. So he was a great worry to his father. Was that all? He felt suddenly abandoned, like the unwanted rag doll he had seen a girl in the apartment building throw down the garbage shute. For the first time in his life he really resented his father. Why couldn't he make the people at the oil company change their minds? Didn't Dad want him on his jobs any more? Even the apartment seemed hostile. It was no longer their home. Mrs. Coutts had already found a new job in the building next door.

"I'll leave the place as clean and empty as when you came," she had promised.

"Empty." Ian hung onto the word. He felt deserted and empty, like reaching for a glass of water with a dreadful thirst and finding nothing inside.

4

Ian's night was troubled with strange dreams. He woke early and jumped out of bed to look down from his seventeenth-floor window. A thick fog heaved and billowed outside, totally erasing the earth below. His father was still asleep.

"I'll run down into the fog," Ian said aloud, listening to see if his words made an echo in the empty apartment. A steady snoring from Mrs. Coutts' room was the only response. He checked his watch with the illuminated hands. It was very early. They probably wouldn't miss him — and he didn't care if they did. He dressed and carefully zipped the door key into the pocket of his old blue jacket. The elevator was empty. The security guard on the main floor hadn't come yet. Ian let himself out through the swinging glass door.

He ran down the steps into a swirling earth-bound cloud and set off down a deserted street. The cloud curled around him, hiding him from the world. Only the call of a foghorn from Lake Michigan came through like the steady beating of a heart.

Ian wished he could really disappear. It wouldn't matter

then that Dad was going to leave him. It wouldn't even matter that he had to live with Aunt Clem. He would just vanish and never go. Dad could stop worrying about him.

But even the fog couldn't erase his uneasy picture of bossy Aunt Clem with her proud upturned chin. Why wouldn't the memory of her words last Christmas go away? "Such a gangly boy," he had heard her say when she thought he was safely out of earshot. "He doesn't seem to have much drive."

Ian's head sagged a little into the fog. The misty air billowed up and down seeming to unearth unpleasant memories from his past. It surged like silent sea waves. Ian kept walking and walking as he swung his arms into the fog. His hands vanished, but not the illuminated hands of his watch, which glowed like cats' eyes in front of him. By now it was 6:45. In fifteen minutes Jack Turner was coming to drive him to Toronto. His Dad should be up now and Mrs. Coutts would be cleaning the apartment.

Aunt Clem's face reappeared in the fog. He remembered a Thanksgiving dinner once at her house when he was a small boy. She had rapped his knuckles with an ivory holder when he wiped jam from his hands onto the white linen serviette. She still treated him like a little boy and he'd have to be on his best behaviour all the time.

"How can Dad send me there?" Ian muttered grimly.

Slowly the morning sun began to burn through the mist. It burned away the folded sheets of fog until they drifted thinner and thinner behind the alleys of houses and into the dark stairwells of the tall apartments.

Ian stood before his own building. A white Volkswagen was parked in front of it and a burly man with short brown hair and tanned face, looking like a football player, opened the door.

"You Ian McDonald?" he called, smoothing down the sleeves of his green sports jacket.

"You must be Jack Turner from Dad's company," Ian answered. "But you're early. I have to say goodbye to Dad."

"All right ... but hurry up. We ought to get going."

Ian escaped into the building and up in the elevator. He rang the apartment doorbell. Mrs. Coutts, flustered and more wrinkled than usual, opened the door.

"Why, there you are. We thought you'd run away. Now

hurry in and see your Dad while I take your bags down to the lobby. And have a good visit with your Auntie."

Andrew McDonald was standing in the living-room.

"Wherever have you been, Ian? I wanted us to have a few minutes together, but now Jack Turner's waiting downstairs." He gripped Ian's hand. "I know you feel pretty miserable, but things will look up when you get there. I'll be lonely too without you. You know that, don't you?"

Ian nodded.

"Toronto's a great city. See if you can't enjoy it. Maybe Aunt Clem will take you up the CN Tower. I'll call her from Inuvik as soon as I know my exact address and phone number."

"And you will come at Christmas, Dad?"

"Yes, of course. We'll see a lot of each other then."

"O.K.... And good luck with the job, Dad."

It wasn't what he really wanted to say.

Ian left and closed the door. It was the end of another home. That hard, hurting lump returned to press against his throat. It was often there now like a stopper holding back tears.

Downstairs the security guard still hadn't appeared and Jack Turner was loading Ian's baggage into the small trunk of the white car. The burly man crawled in beside him and began fussing again with the sleeves of his coat. His fingers curled like fat sausages over the steering wheel, and he looked with distaste at the eastern sky where dark clouds were beginning to cover the sun.

"Looks like the weather's going to turn nasty." Jack Turner squirmed about in his seat, almost filling it, then roared the motor. "I've got a meeting in Toronto tonight and I've got to make it on time. I didn't really need a passenger, but you just sit tight and we'll be fine."

When they reached the suburbs of Chicago drops of rain began to splash against the windows. Turner flicked on the windshield wiper.

"Blast this weather," he said and turned the car onto the speeding highway. He twisted the radio knob and found a noisy band.

"He doesn't want to talk to me," Ian thought miserably.

The outskirts flashed by — more houses, apartments, office buildings. Turner was a fast driver. The rain was steady now. It was getting darker. Turner glanced at his watch.

"It's only eight o'clock and it looks like midnight. If we don't make Toronto before dark I'm in trouble."

Ian didn't care about his trouble. The windshield wiper whipped back and forth, fighting the rain.

At last they were in the country and against the steady pounding of the rain Ian fell into a long, long sleep. When he woke, they were already in Detroit, creeping behind thick rows of cars. Dreary factories with fenced-in, cement-covered fields were on either side. Turner fidgetted nervously over their slow progress. The swells of smoke from the factories muddied the windshield and sent Ian into a fit of sneezing. He found he didn't have a handkerchief and had to wipe his nose on the sleeve of his blue jacket. Turner looked disdainful but said nothing. Why did his father send him with such a sullen, unfriendly man?

Ian scrunched into the far corner of the seat. But he didn't stay there long. In front of him rose the Ambassador Suspension Bridge swinging across the Detroit River into Canada. They drove onto it. The sun broke through briefly and the twisted wire-rope cables sparkled like strands of silver thread, lifting them into the sky. The cables reached upward in loops as gracefully as the swooping wings of a seagull. Ian held his breath and wondered why he and Dad had always crossed through the tunnel under the river. The bridge suspended them above the smoke and muddy rain. Ian's head cleared and he could breathe deeply again. All borders should be crossed by bridges, he decided: they joined countries together instead of separating them.

But Jack Turner didn't seem to care about the bridge. He growled at the slow-moving cars and trucks. He was still growling as they came to the customs booth where a uniformed woman asked her routine questions.

"U.S. citizen," Turner said. "Business trip to Toronto."

"Is the boy your son?" the woman asked.

"My son? That's a laugh," Turner scoffed.

"It's a laugh for me too." Ian scowled, not caring at all what Jack Turner thought.

The woman turned to Ian.

"My father is a Canadian citizen," Ian said clearly. "My mother was an American." Ian paused. He never liked saying his mother was dead. Was he supposed to tell the woman? Maybe she didn't care. "I'm going to visit my aunt in Toronto." He refused to say "live with my aunt".

5

Ian liked entering Canada. It was less crowded, with great silent spaces leading north. He conjured up images of majestic pine trees pointing skyward, natural and undisturbed. Even Jack Turner seemed to relax as they broke through into the countryside.

By now it was nearly one o'clock. Turner pulled over in front of a drive-in restaurant and ordered hamburgers and Coca Cola to go. Ian was hungry and for the first time since starting on the trip felt grateful to his companion. As they munched their food, Turner too seemed in better humour.

They sped along Canada's fast-moving highway 401. Steady splashes of rain hit the windows making a blur of the highway and the oncoming cars with their puddles of light. A swaying tree bent from its trunk in the now furious wind.

"Hadn't you better slow down?" Ian said grimly to Turner. "My Dad would never speed through a storm like this."

Turner didn't answer. He reached for a rag under the seat and wiped moisture from the windows.

"Got to have a little air in here." He rolled down his window, pushing his foot steadily against the gas pedal. The wind swished through the opening, sending loose papers flying. An Ontario road map, lying on the dashboard, crackled upward and sailed out into the storm. Turner grabbed into the empty wind and groaned. "I'm beginning to think this trip is jinxed. We're behind time, it hasn't stopped raining and now the map blows out the window."

"Serve you right," Ian thought. "I hope we get lost." He settled back angrily into the corner of his seat.

They drove on steadily without speaking. It seemed like hours to Ian. The rain pounded harder and the wind began sweeping loose branches and soggy leaves over the road.

"Better fasten your seat belt tight," Turner finally warned, still not slowing down. "The sign back there said it's illegal not to wear them in this country."

Ian tugged at his belt, trying to tighten it, but he was so thin that the buckle fell limp in front of him.

A sizzling fuse of lightning zig-zagged through the sky as though heading for a stick of dynamite. It exploded with crackling thunder. The shock pounded into the middle of Ian's stomach and jerked Jack Turner's arm, sending the speeding Volkswagen into a skid that almost caused them to crash into a traffic jam in front of them. One car did slide off the road into a ditch.

Ian bit his lips to hold back a cry. What was wrong with this man and his driving? Dad would have pulled over to the side and stopped a long time ago. It wasn't safe to go this fast on a wet road and with blinding lightning. Turner must be crazy.

The traffic ahead of them seemed to be barely moving. Turner was forced to slow down.

"Must be a bad accident," Turner muttered impatiently as he spotted a police car ahead. He shook a clenched fist in the direction of the stalled cars.

A lot of good that does, Ian thought with contempt.

Two policemen began to motion with their flashlights.

"Blast! Looks like they're diverting us onto sideroads," Turner said, straining to see through the hammering rain on the windshield. He turned off and they inched forward until their headlights picked out a green and white sign that read "Waterloo County". Turner jerked the car into another turn. The rain poured from an earth-black sky.

"We'll find a town and get some directions for Toronto," Turner mumbled, bending forward over the steering wheel and glaring at the unyielding water. The road narrowed. Ian looked out the side window away from the driver. A village or two whipped by with feeble lights as though folded up for shelter inside some huge umbrella. There was no warmth and no welcome in any of them. September corn with ripe, dry leaves crackled and danced in flashes of lightning. Soon the villages disappeared into mile after mile of wide black fields guarded by swinging trees. Turner seemed ill at ease with the lack of lights and signs and of anyone to ask directions. He pressed steadily against the gas pedal.

Is he afraid of the storm, Ian wondered. Does he think he can drive away from it? He looked at the speedometer. Turner was driving at over seventy miles an hour.

"You ought to slow down," Ian warned.

Turner wasn't listening.

The road curved abruptly. It seemed more and more lonely and forlorn. It was narrower, too, with wet gravel paths on either side. Ian hoped that Turner would stay in the middle and that no cars would come plunging towards them. The headlights sprayed a dim yellow path ahead, but the rain formed a curtain that blocked it and Ian could see only a short distance.

Without warning, a strange object appeared on the shoulder of the road to the right. It was a large orange triangle. Ian blinked. Was it real? He'd never seen anything like it before.

Turner was alarmed. "What's that orange sign? It's moving."

"I don't know." Ian's vision blurred. He leaned back and twisted the seat belt tighter. The triangle became a splash of orange in front of him.

"Watch out!" Ian yelled.

Jack Turner lifted his foot off the gas pedal and smashed it onto the brake. The car wheels screamed with skidding and headed for the triangle as though it were a target. Ian's feet dug into the floorboards of the small car. Turner's face swung forward, white as a snowman's with deep hollow eyes.

The car took a strange spin into a puddle of mud and veered to the left away from the triangle. Then Ian felt the rear of the car fishtail as Turner attempted to correct the slide. Suddenly the front bumper thudded into something large and brown directly in front of the car. The orange triangle at the back exploded into sprays of cracking, spinning colour.

An unearthly scream pierced the air. Ian cringed. The impact jarred him and his bones felt shaken from their sockets. Jack Turner's head snapped backward. Ian could hear it crack against the side window.

The brown object seemed to ooze over the car as the hood of the Volkswagen crumpled towards the windshield. Ian thought of his luggage being smashed in the front trunk. The engine sputtered and stopped. Ian's seat belt bit into his stomach.

The brown object began to slip away from the car and slowly sank onto the ground. The long, bony legs of an animal kicked from its sides. Then they stiffened and fell like broken poles into a cornfield. Wood cracked around a huge black box with wooden wheels beneath it. As the animal fell, a man and boy were thrown head first from the box. They landed in the cornfield.

"We've hit a horse!" Jack Turner's voice was thin and reedy. "It's a horse and buggy!"

It *was* a horse. Ian could see it now, lying stiff and quiet on the ground. He looked out of the cracked car window with disbelief.

"We've knocked all the life out of him."

6

The boy who had been thrown from the black box was bending over the dead horse. He was crying and trying to lift the heavy head. The man struggled to free his legs from under one of the buggy wheels and then dragged himself by his hands slowly from the cornfield towards the boy and the horse. His legs did not move but stretched out awkwardly behind him like useless strands of rope. He ran his fingers over the horse's eyes and closed them. Ian could see that his face was contorted with pain.

Ian rubbed his own eyes. Were the man and the boy real? They wore black hats with wide round brims. A frame of neatly trimmed brown hair beneath their hats had the appearance of an upside-down bowl. Their pants were baggy and held up with suspenders. The black box that had been pulled by the dead horse tipped forward over two crushed wheels.

The scene before Ian was eerie, for the wind had stopped blowing, the rain had ceased and the air was suddenly dry. The black clouds parted and there was a strange late afternoon sunlight that was almost supernatural.

The man tried to lift the boy gently at the elbow, his long brown beard brushing over the dead horse. It wasn't a fashionable beard like those of some of the men in Dad's office. It was full and long like the picture of great-grandfather McDonald that hung in Aunt Clem's house.

Why were they so silent, Ian wondered. Weren't they going to shout at them about killing the horse? Ian pushed against the car door and it opened. He felt sore and stiff when he stepped outside, but he wasn't hurt. The man on the ground, however, was badly injured. Ian moved to help him.

Then he heard a groan on the opposite side of the Volkswagen. He turned to see Jack Turner stumbling out of the car and trying to stand by the crumpled hood. The sleeve of his green jacket was ripped and the glass on his watch was splintered. He leaned forward, trying to appraise the wrecked buggy and the dead horse.

25

"I suppose you have insurance?" He directed his question at the man with the beard who was hunched up miserably on the ground. At the same time Turner tried to pull together his ripped jacket and clear away the congestion in his throat.

"Insurance!" Ian wanted to scream. Why did Jack Turner ask about this now? Couldn't he try to help the injured man? Couldn't he say he was sorry that he had been driving like a maniac?

The bearded man lifted his head quietly. His expression was one of gentle sadness. He winced as he tried to move his legs; he could not stand.

"I don't have insurance," he said simply. "Our religion doesn't allow it. We take care of our own people."

"No insurance!" Jack Turner's voice cracked and he looked at the man with disbelief. Ian was also puzzled. What kind of religion would oppose insurance?

But this was no time for questions. The road began to fill with lights, for the sky had grown dark again with storm clouds, even though the rain had stopped. A police car careen-ed into view with its spinning top blinking. Someone must have reported the accident. The car pulled up beside the broken buggy and two officers in uniform jumped out. One of them ran to the bearded man who now lay on the ground with his eyes closed. The officer covered him quickly with a heavy blanket.

"Ambulance!" he shouted to his partner.

"One's already on the way," came the reply.

Ian heard horses' hooves clopping along the gravel side of the road and looking up he saw that it was another horse and black buggy. Where was he? Who were these strange people who rode about the country in horses and buggies?

People started to appear from all directions. A man in shorts with two small boys asked if he could help. Two teenage boys ran to the horse and pressed their ears against his chest, listening for a heart beat. They shook their heads. The second policeman quickly pushed them away and motioned for another police car that had just arrived to set up a road block. The car beeped with short, urgent warning sounds.

Ian was confused. Who should he help? What should he do? He was startled by a sudden stern voice from behind.

"What's the meaning of speeding in weather like this? You must have braked violently or you'd both be smashed to pieces." A red-faced policeman was confronting Jack Turner.

Turner didn't answer.

"Your name and address." The policeman was gruff.

Then Ian heard questions being asked about him.

"Who's the boy?"

"Ian McDonald." Jack Turner was co-operating now. "I was taking the boy to visit his aunt in Toronto. His father left today on a trip."

"Where's the boy's mother," the policeman's voice rasped.

"Dead," Turner answered in a matter-of-fact way.

Ian was shocked. Dad always spoke of his mother with respect — as if she was a great lady. A hollow place in his chest always began to ache when he thought about her. It was weird. He'd never even known her. Ian shivered. He tried pulling his jacket shut and then remembered that the zipper was broken.

There were women now in big black bonnets and long blue dresses walking around the buggies and the cars. One of them ran to the bearded man and then put her arm around the boy whose horse had been killed. The women near Ian talked in low voices to each other in a language that sounded rather like the Dutch he'd learned to speak in Amsterdam.

A kindly looking woman with gold-rimmed glasses came up to Ian and wrapped a black shawl around his shoulders.

"The boy is cold and wet," the bonnetted woman said, now in English, to the policeman. "Why don't we take him to the farm until all this trouble is settled?"

Jack Turner lurched forward in protest.

"That's a good idea." The policeman seemed to be calming down.

"Don't worry about the boy," he said. "Horse and Buggy Jonah and his son Ezra have a fine place. The Benders are two of the best farmers around here. You better give me the phone number of the aunt in Toronto."

Turner fumbled inside the pocket of his torn sports coat and handed a paper to the policeman. As he did this, his hand dropped suddenly and his body tumbled to the ground.

"He's fainted! Take him over to the police car."

27

The ominous whine of an ambulance siren filled the air, zeroing in closer and closer. When it arrived the road block parted to admit the white enamelled vehicle. Two attendants stepped out of it carrying a stretcher. A third followed with a large gray blanket. They headed towards the bearded man and knelt beside him for a while, one of them raising his head gently, while the other two examined his injuries. Ian watched them move him gingerly onto the stretcher. At this point the woman with the black bonnet and gold-rimmed glasses came up to him. She looked into his face.

"Is the man who was driving the car a relative of yours?" she asked.

Her voice was plain and kind. It somehow calmed Ian. He felt like he was grabbing onto a big, sturdy handle.

"I met him for the first time this morning." Ian's voice quivered. Surely he wasn't going to cry in front of a stranger?

"Do you have some bags?" She searched in the car.

"They're smashed in the trunk," Ian replied.

"Then come along," she said.

The woman lifted him up onto the front seat of a square black buggy. Very soon the boy whose horse had been killed was sitting beside him. He was trying to hold back his sobs, but was still wiping tears from his eyes. Someone put a heavy blanket over their legs with a rubber cover to keep out the rain.

7

The rain began to fall again. This time it pattered gently against the sides and top of the black buggy and over the rubber-covered blanket. The woman and the boy warmed Ian on either side. The black clouds lifted in the west allowing escape for a few sun rays to light the road.

Ian took a deep breath of air, so fresh with earth smells that he wanted to hold it inside him. He'd never ridden behind a horse with a swishing black tail before. It didn't need steering or guiding. The woman held the reins lightly in her lap.

The sunlight spread peacefully over the freshly-washed countryside and the nervous, beeping flashes of the police car faded. The woman and the boy spoke softly in English combined with their Dutch-sounding language. The jogging rhythm of the horse and buggy became as soothing as a rocking chair. Ian was glad they didn't question him.

It almost seems like I'm riding backwards in time, he thought, and then he began wishing the impossible — that he could go so far back in time he would forget about Dad going to the Northwest Territories without him; that he would never hear of Jack Turner and the accident again; that he would ride away from Aunt Clem forever. He looked at the open space under the rain cloud in the sky and wished that it would shut down over them like the lid of a bread-box. For some unexplainable reason he leaned his head against the woman's clean-smelling shoulder. The horse swished its black tail and trotted steadily ahead. But none of Ian's wishing could erase from his memory the dead horse. The boy who had cried over its brown head sat silently beside him.

The lid of black clouds lifted higher and the early evening sun sparkled over the wet earth. It was a moment of welcome, for the buggy turned into a long lane at the end of which stretched a big white clapboard house. High maple trees stood around it with clusters of red and orange leaves in bursts of regal splendour.

Two small barefoot girls with long purple dresses stood in the doorway. Their heads were covered with tight-fitting black caps and every strand of hair was tucked carefully beneath them.

"Sarah — Mary," the woman beside Ian called out in greeting. The girls started for the buggy and then, seeing Ian, ran back towards the door and stood shyly behind it.

This wasn't real. It was a movie, Ian decided, with people in period dress. He felt he was being transported backwards in time, just like once in hospital, when he had his broken arm set. Someone had given him gas and asked him to count backward from twenty-five. Gradually the numbers had been replaced by a humming of bees in his ears, octaves above their normal pitch, circling, buzzing and carrying him back and back, further and further.

A windmill spun around and around near an ambling barn with its doors spread wide at one end for the horses and cows strolling home from a purple meadow. A bank of earth led to the enormous barn door on the second floor where a farm wagon was entering drawn by two sturdy horses.

This farm and its people could have existed as far back as 1775, Ian decided, when some of the McDonalds had fled to Canada during the American revolution because they were loyal to Britain. Pictures of these relatives filled the walls of Aunt Clem's home: the women wore long dresses, most men had sweeping beards, and the children were dressed in caps with chubby feet poking below billowing skirts and baggy trousers.

The black-bonnetted woman beside him, Ian thought, could be a pioneer Loyalist with her brown hair pulled tightly back from her face. Her expression was determined but gentle. Her blue eyes, behind the gold-rimmed glasses, were severe but warm.

She drew in the reins and the horse stopped obediently.

"Unhitch the horse, Reuben," she said softly. "The police will come later and tell us about Ezra."

"But Aunt Lydia," Reuben's voice choked, "shouldn't I keep Prince hitched to get Momma? And who will bury Star?"

"Your Mom has gone to the hospital with your Pop," she said simply. "Already the Nafsingers and the Gingerich brothers know about the accident. They will take care of Star and the smashed buggy. Let's just thank God that you and your father and Ian here are alive. Star saved your lives. The car hit him instead of the buggy."

The accident came rushing back and Ian felt slightly sick again. Maybe now this boy Reuben with his bowl of brown hair and his steady brown eyes would protest about Turner's car killing his horse.

But it didn't happen. Aunt Lydia jumped from the buggy as easily as stepping from a stool. Then she held Ian's arm while he jumped too.

"Mary — Sarah," she called to the red-cheeked little girls,

31

quaintly old in their long plain purple dresses with matching aprons. They didn't hear for they dashed from their hiding place and ran to the barn. Soon they reappeared with Reuben who carried the smallest one, Sarah, in his arms.

They chattered to each other in the strange language that Ian couldn't understand. The little girls cried softly and wiped their eyes with the long sleeves of their dresses. When Ian heard the word "Star" he knew Reuben had told them about the horse.

"We speak 'Pennsylvania Dutch' at home, Ian," Aunt Lydia explained offhandedly as they all walked through a large back door. "If there's something you don't understand, ask me and I'll tell you in English."

A row of hooks along the wall held bonnets, wide-brimmed hats, shawls and coats and on the floor beneath them was a neat row of black rubber boots in every size. Ian hung his blue jacket with the broken zipper on one of the hooks.

It became dark again outside, for another storm cloud covered the sun, but a pleasant soft light spread over the roomy farmhouse kitchen. Ian saw that it came from a kerosene lamp hanging from a hook above the long kitchen table. Another woman, maybe about twenty-four Ian guessed, stirred with a wooden spoon a large pot of food cooking on a wide black stove. She bent over, picked up a split log from a box nearby and shoved it inside near the oven. Ian remembered stories of his great-great-grandmother McDonald having a wood-burning stove, but nobody used them today. It was too much work. Besides, there was gas and electricity. When did these people think they were living? One of the girls opened a cupboard drawer and pulled out a plate of butter and thick slices of home-made bread. There didn't seem to be a refrigerator. How did they keep milk cold, and eggs? A hundred questions darted around Ian's mind.

The young woman who cooked answered to "Becky". She knew about Star and the accident and nodded sadly towards Reuben. She too was dressed in clothes that belonged in a history book. Ian noticed how straight she stood before the stove with her bare feet standing firmly on the wooden floor. She smiled at Ian and then shook his hand with one vigorous up-and-down motion.

She's beautiful, Ian thought. Her cheeks were flushed from the cooking stove and her dark eyes and hair, tucked beneath a white cap, shone like polished mahogany.

A side door opened and a short man with broad shoulders stood inside the room. His hair was a bowl of white and his long white beard fell softly over a dark blue shirt. His baggy black coat and pants were exactly like Reuben's and were held up with the same kind of suspenders.

"Grossdoddy!" the children called out.

"Jonah," Aunt Lydia said.

Ian remembered what the policeman had said. This must be Horse and Buggy Jonah Bender, the best farmer in the county. The old man spoke quietly in Pennsylvania Dutch and then, looking at Ian, changed to English.

"It's a strange name you have, Ian," he said. "It's not one we know."

He shook Ian's hand with the same pump-handle vigour that Becky had used.

"This is a hard time for you. Your father is far away, I hear, and you don't have a mother."

His eyes were even bluer than Aunt Lydia's, but more direct. Ian didn't know whether to answer. The same question persisted. Were these people real? Maybe he was dreaming after all. They focussed clearly and then blurred, like bad reception on a television screen. He very much wanted them to be there. He didn't want a knob to turn them off and have them disappear.

Grandfather Jonah drew closer and stood between him and Reuben.

"You've both been in an accident." He continued to speak quietly. "But I thank God that you weren't hurt.... Now let's wash and eat some supper."

He led them to a corner of the kitchen where a pump with a long handle stood over a wash basin.

"I think I'd like to go to your bathroom instead," Ian said. He was surprised that he could speak, he had been silent for so long.

Jonah laughed. Even Reuben smiled.

"Ach well," the old man chuckled, "you don't know much about us yet. *Das alt gebrauch* — we think the old ways are the

33

best. Our bathroom, as you say it, Ian, is outside. . . . Take him to the outhouse, Reuben, then come back and wash your hands at the pump and we'll eat."

Ian was incredulous. No bathroom! But of course, this would go with being a pioneer. Or maybe they were just pretending to live 200 years ago. Could they be poor?

When they returned, everyone was seated at the table. The girls sat with Aunt Lydia and Rebecca along one side, and Jonah and Reuben sat on the other. An empty seat at the end of the table must be for the father, Ezra, Ian thought, and another empty place beside the girls must be for the mother, Susie. But why was no-one sitting in the chair between Reuben and Grossdoddy? It wasn't for Ian. He was given a stool at the far end of the men's row.

8

Rebecca and Aunt Lydia carried bowls of steaming food from the stove to the table. Those gathered around it were calm and quiet. Ian wondered why no-one was seeking revenge for the dead horse and the wrecked buggy. Shouldn't they be bitter that Ezra was in hospital because of a reckless driver?

Instead all of them sat at the table and bowed their heads for silent prayer. Ian, rather puzzled, bowed his head too. He and Dad prayed before Christmas and Thanksgiving dinners at Aunt Clem's. But someone always spoke and the prayers were short. The long pendulum of a big wall clock ticked loudly. Ian twisted his head to look at it. Five minutes passed. Grandfather Jonah cleared his throat, heads lifted and everyone began to reach for the dishes of food and fill their own plates. There was meat, gravy, creamed potatoes.

"The tomatoes and green beans are just picked from the garden," Aunt Lydia said to Ian.

Ian couldn't believe his appetite. He filled every space on his plate. Then he filled it a second time. The others at the table seemed pleased that he was so hungry. He didn't notice that they ate very little.

When Ian thought they had finished, Rebecca brought a

large pie bubbling with brown sugar syrup over sliced cooked apples. She cut all the pieces long and wide. There weren't any pie plates. Ian watched the others. They wiped their dinner plates clean with a slice of homemade bread to make a place for their dessert. Not a bad idea, he thought. He took a second piece of pie and drank a steaming cup of sweet mint tea.

The meal ended as abruptly as it began with all heads bowed in silence. This time, however, the family knelt beside their chairs and benches. Even little Sarah slipped from her high chair to the floor and folded her hands near Mary's. Another five minutes ticked away on the clock. Ian sat stiffly on his stool, feeling embarrassed. Whatever their religion was, he didn't belong to it and he wasn't going to take part. He waited to be scolded, but no one paid any attention.

Jonah began reading from a German Bible. At the end of a page he changed to English and read, "Blessed are they that mourn, for they shall be comforted." Then in a more informal voice but still in English, the old white-haired man said softly, "Our faith will get us through this hard time. The hard times help us to appreciate the good times."

Jonah coughed and all the family rose and took their seats again at the table. What were they thinking during their silence, Ian wondered. Were they really expecting God to get them through the trouble caused by the accident and not do anything about it themselves? He wondered if he should stay here. Maybe he should call Aunt Clem and try to go to Toronto tonight. Then he found himself yawning. The day stretched out endlessly and he was tired.

He'd never eaten so much food at one meal in his life. The long trip by horse and buggy in the clean, rain-washed air, the quiet kitchen with the red glow from the burning wood, the soft light from the kerosene lamp had made him sleepy. He wanted to stay in this old-fashioned home and crawl under the blankets in one of their beds. He would have liked a shower, but how could he take one if there wasn't a proper bathroom? He really didn't care. If they didn't bathe, he wouldn't either. He didn't feel at all like a stranger.

The Benders did not seem to be embarrassed that things were done "in the old way" in Jonah's home. Ian looked

35

around him and wondered what Aunt Clem would say about the bare floors and the windows without curtains. The big room, off the kitchen, had almost no furniture — just a rocking chair, a long couch with a head rest, an old sewing machine that pedalled and a few straight chairs. There was no television, no radio, no reading lamp and only one small shelf of books and papers. There were no photographs and nothing on the walls. But in one corner of the shelf Ian noticed a bright bowl of deep pink zinnias. Aunt Lydia glanced at them now and then and smiled.

Jonah stood at the head of the table and began giving directions in English. His blue eyes searched Ian's face.

"Things are a little mixed up here with Ezra and Susie at the hospital," he said. "I'm an old man now and not as strong as I used to be, but I'll take charge until Ezra comes home."

He turned to Aunt Lydia. "The Gingerich brothers came over and did the evening chores, but they forgot to put the sows inside the pens with the baby pigs. Listen. They're hungry." Grossdoddy smiled, then he nodded at Ian. "You go with Reuben to the barn."

"Me!" Ian was astonished. Was he supposed to help Reuben? He'd never been near a live pig.

Reuben took his black coat from the hook near the kitchen table. Ian grabbed his blue jacket and pulled it on. The kitchen had become a hive of activity. Aunt Lydia pulled a rocking chair near the stove and settled into it with a ball of black yarn and a half-knit mitten. The girls stood on their bare tiptoes lifting dishes from the table to a counter nearby. Rebecca

poured boiling water from a heavy tea-kettle on the stove into a pan that stood in a sink with no drain or faucet. Mary pulled a chair from the table and climbed onto it, ready to wash the dishes.

"We better hurry," Reuben called to Ian from the open door. Ian could plainly hear the squealing pigs now.

The night was dark, with bright stars and no moon in sight, but Reuben swung streams of light from two lanterns that he carried. Ian followed him. When they reached the barn, Reuben handed Ian the lanterns and pulled back the heavy door. They stepped inside. Ian had never been in a barn filled with animals. A cat jumped from a ceiling beam and rubbed against his legs. Chickens clucked from another beam, aiming their sharp beaks in his direction. The chorus of clucks, miaows, neighs and moos was exciting. Imagine the fun it would be to have all these animals to take care of. Ian envied Reuben. With a pang of sadness, he remembered Angel and wished he could have kept him.

He followed Reuben behind a row of cows' legs and swishing tails. What if one of them kicked? Ian moved close to the wall. The animals munched into a trough with single-minded concentration. The lantern light spread over the backs of two strong work-horses. Their great hooves pawed at the straw on the floor, their scraping horseshoes as big as the weights in the school gymnasium in Chicago. Reuben walked close to one of them in his bare feet and stroked its head. Ian kept well back. Wasn't Reuben afraid?

They came to an empty stall and Reuben stopped in front of it. "Star lived here," he said slowly.

The accident rose in front of Ian like an accusing finger. How could he tell this strange old-fashioned boy how much he wished Star were still alive and standing in the barn swishing his tail. He wanted desperately to say that he was not responsible for Jack Turner's wild driving, that he was sorry about Ezra and that he too had felt like crying when Star's kicking legs fell to the ground and he died. But no words came.

A big collie jumped between the boys, staying close to Reuben and wagging his tail joyfully. Reuben rubbed his ear. Ian touched the dog's soft, warm nose. This was just the kind of dog he would like to own.

37

"Star was killed by a car," Reuben said to the collie, and Ian felt ashamed.

The boys hurried towards the pig pen where squealing, grunting and banging noises had become an explosion. How could one young boy take care of such an uproar?

"Hold the lantern, Ian," Reuben said calmly. "Climb up that post. The sows can't knock you down. It's too bad Poppa isn't here. He just talks to the pigs and they settle down."

The post Ian was to climb was outside the pen. He was relieved. He looked down into the pen at three of the biggest pigs he had ever seen. They were oversized sand-coloured balloons, blown up to breaking point and weighted down with heavy flesh that sent them swaying from side to side, scraping and bumping into one another. Reuben jumped into the midst of them with his strong bare feet.

"Jenny goes in the first pen," he shouted, kicking her in the side and shoving her wet slippery snout with his hand. He slid open a door and she waddled through. Twelve baby pigs rushed at her like an ocean wave. They trampled over each other's heads to feed from their mother. She rolled peacefully onto the straw-covered floor, not caring that two of the smallest pigs were squealing beneath her.

"Dimples goes in here," Reuben called out again, shoving at the second sow.

"And now for Rascal. She's the most trouble of all."

Rascal was faster on her feet than the others and raced around the pen several times before entering the door that Reuben held open for her. Ian was amazed. Reuben was no bigger than he, yet he had no fear of these ponderous, snorting animals.

"Don't they ever bite?" Ian asked.

"Sometimes." Reuben smiled cautiously, as though wondering how friendly he should be with Ian. Then he relaxed. "We ride Rascal when Pop is out of the barn. She sends us flying. John is better...."

Reuben's smile vanished.

"John must be your brother," Ian offered. "That's who the empty seat at the table belongs to."

"I can't talk about John." Reuben was abrupt. He took the lantern from Ian and walked slowly behind the animal stalls.

The openness of a few moments before was gone as though a door had closed between them, taking the old-fashioned boy into a room where Ian wasn't allowed. Had John committed some serious crime?

The barn warmed with the breath of animals ready for sleep. The cat curled beneath the drooping head of a tired work-horse. The collie stretched over a pile of straw and nuzzled his nose against the cat's soft fur. The chickens buried their sharp beaks under blankets of feathers. The squeals from the pigs were hushed to contented grunts. Night was for sleeping and Reuben turned down the wick and blew out the flame from one of the lanterns. Ian followed him out of doors.

Ian yawned a second time. Surely now they would go to bed. They had almost reached the kitchen door when two car lights leapt into the darkness from the end of the farm lane. Reuben and Ian ran back to the yard. Jonah appeared, then Aunt Lydia with the girls behind her.

"It's the policeman, Tom Higgins," Jonah told them. "He'll have news about Ezra." The lights bumped up and down with the ruts in the road, then dimmed as the car slowed and finally stopped near Jonah.

A stout red-faced man in uniform stuck his head from the open window of his car.

"Is that you, Horse and Buggy Jonah?" he called out.

"Yah," Jonah answered walking towards the car window.

"The news isn't good about Ezra," the policeman said. "His leg is smashed. They may have to operate. Susie is staying with him in the hospital."

The family in the yard were silent.

"We are going to fine Turner heavily. He may lose his driver's licence." The policeman spoke directly to Jonah. "I know you won't press charges for the loss of your horse and buggy."

"Yah, that's right," the old man agreed.

Ian wanted to object. Jonah had every right to make Jack Turner pay for the damage he had caused. But he kept quiet. It was impossible to understand these people.

"It's a bad time for an accident with the harvest and all the work." The policeman spoke this time more as a friend.

"Yah, but we'll manage." Jonah folded his arms over his

39

stomach. "Our people will help. It will be the hardest on Ezra. He won't like it in the hospital. He'll miss the farm and his family."

"About the boy." The policeman nodded towards Ian. "Turner is still quite shaken but the doctor thinks he will be all right by morning. We called the aunt in Toronto and told her that her nephew was on the best farm in the county." The officer wiped his head with a handkerchief. "She was pretty upset. If she hadn't been in bed with the flu she would have come here at once to get him. She's going to telephone in the morning."

"Yah?" Jonah smiled. "She'll have a hard time doing that."

"I forgot." The policeman slapped the side of the car and laughed. "You don't have a telephone."

No telephone! Ian was overjoyed. He didn't want Aunt Clem breaking into this peaceful, old-time world.

Aunt Lydia intervened in her brisk way. "It's very late," she said, shooing the children inside the house. "Ian can sleep upstairs in the boys' room with Reuben. It's warmer to sleep together."

"But I've never slept with anybody in my life," Ian objected.

Aunt Lydia didn't listen, for upstairs in the clean but barren boys' room there was only one large bed.

Ten minutes later Ian burrowed deep into its soft warmth. Reuben was already sound asleep. His back was a small, reassuring heater beside Ian. Yet how did Reuben feel, he wondered, sleeping with a boy who rode in the car that killed his horse. Remorse tugged at Ian. He could easily wake Reuben now and say something. But the words still wouldn't come.

Ian felt a little guilty, too, about Aunt Clem. She would be worried. It was all very well pretending he had slipped 200 years backwards in time and had lost Aunt Clem someplace through the centuries. But Ian realized the Bender farm wasn't an escape. There was a telephone box at the end of the farm lane, there were modern cars driving in and out of the farm lane, and he'd even seen an aeroplane zooming through the sky when he and Reuben came out of the barn. But for some reason he didn't understand yet, these quiet, friendly, religious people were living their long-ago past in the present. They weren't

40

just pretending to be old-fashioned like the Dutch people at the tulip festival in Amsterdam each spring. They wanted to be different.

The day's turmoil finally caught up with Ian and he slept.

9

When Ian woke it was early morning. A faint light rimmed the windows around the pulled-down shades. There were no curtains to keep it out. Where was he? Had Dad left for the North yet? Where was Mrs. Coutts? Ian sat up in bed, saw Reuben beside him and then remembered. A crackling noise came from downstairs. Aunt Lydia must be lighting the wood-burning stove. The clip-clop beat of horses' hooves sounded through the half-opened bedroom window, followed by the scraping noise of steel-rimmed buggy wheels. It could be the neighbours coming to help. A rooster crowed and a horse neighed shrilly from the barn.

Aunt Lydia, in a long green dress with a black apron, appeared at the bedroom door. Her hair was neatly parted in the middle and tucked under a small white cap. She still wore the gold-rimmed glasses. What would Reuben and Aunt Lydia think if he told them that yesterday morning he got out of bed on the seventeenth floor of a highrise apartment in the city of Chicago where the only morning sounds were the humming traffic far below and the occasional roar of an aeroplane overhead, and where the only animal he was allowed was a tame white rat? Ian chuckled. They probably wouldn't believe him.

This morning Aunt Lydia was barefoot like the children. Ian had the same feeling of well-being about her that he had had when he first met her. Outgoing, honest, without any pretending, she would be as dependable as the sturdy clapboard farmhouse.

"It's time to get up, Reuben and Ian," she said quietly. Reuben stirred sleepily but didn't resist. Both legs slid over the side of the bed even though his eyes were closed.

"And Ian," Aunt Lydia called as she turned to go down the stairs, "I've put some of Reuben's clothes on the chair for you.

41

Your pants and shirt are torn and dirty. The zipper on your jacket needs mending. I'll have them ready for you by Sunday morning."

Ian rebelled. Why should he wear loose baggy pants instead of blue jeans. He was a visitor. He wasn't one of these people. What would his Chicago school friends think if they saw him in a lot of home-made clothes? Even Tony would laugh. He could just hear him: "Trying to pull yourself up by your suspenders, Ian?" But Reuben didn't seem to think there was anything unusual.

Ian searched the room. He had no choice. If he didn't want to run around all day in a night-shirt, he had to wear these clothes. Aunt Lydia had already disappeared with his dirty ones. Ian watched Reuben carefully. Together they pulled on bright home-made shirts without collars. Reuben rolled up the long sleeves and Ian followed. Suspenders were already fastened to the dark, heavy-duty pants that closed in front with a flap that buttoned along the waist.

"Why don't the pants have zippers, Reuben?"

"Zippers?" Reuben seemed puzzled. "Mom always makes our pants this way. Zippers are for the English."

"English?" Ian queried, but Reuben shrugged it off.

Ian was surprised that the pants were loose and comfortable. Reuben ignored his shoes, so Ian kicked his under a chair, even though he'd never gone barefoot before. Reuben walked to a small table in the corner of the room, picked up a hairbrush on top of it and smoothed his hair around his face with two strokes. Ian did the same.

"We look like brothers." Reuben smiled shyly as they raced down the stairs. "But I don't have red hair."

Ian was surprised by this hesitant friendliness.

"I'll give you some of my hair," he joked.

Jonah was waiting for them, wearing his wide-brimmed black felt hat and a short black coat that was fastened in the front with hooks and eyes. His feet were heavy with black shoes whose tops came over his ankles.

"There was a ring around the moon last night, boys," he greeted them. "A sure sign of more rain."

He hoisted his cane over his shoulder and walked outside with one hand on Reuben's arm.

42

"I'm an old man now —" Jonah hobbled along as the three of them strolled towards the barn "— and my working days are over. But I can tell a new boy how to do the chores."

Ian groaned inwardly. The only thing he knew about chores was that you did them before breakfast. What would he do if Jonah asked him to milk a cow? He wouldn't even know where to look for eggs from the chickens. He didn't know what the horses and cows ate. Why hadn't they taught him farming at one of his schools?

Jonah waved his hand towards a horse and buggy tied to a post beside the barn.

"Gravy Dan came over to clean the manure from the stalls. He'll spread it over the fields before we plough."

"Gravy Dan?" Ian asked.

"Yah well, it's just that among us Amish," Jonah explained, "many people have the same name. Three Dan Nafsingers live on the road. There has to be some way to tell them apart. Gravy Dan got his nickname when he poured gravy instead of cream into his coffee at a threshing dinner."

"There must be a lot of Jonah Benders," Ian said, remembering the name 'Horse and Buggy Jonah'.

"That's right," Reuben answered this time. "One drives a car with black bumpers; one owns a blue Ford; and Grossdoddy is the only one with a horse and buggy who is Amish. But there's only one Ezra Bender," Reuben added quickly, "and that's my Pop."

"You said Amish," Ian questioned. "What's that?"

"That's who we are," Jonah smiled. "Some people call us the 'Plain People'. Yah, well, you never met any Amish before. If you can stay with us for a while, you'll meet plenty."

"But that's not an explanation," Ian objected.

"Well," Jonah sighed, "it's a long story. I'll tell you a little now and more later." He continued working as he talked, filling the animal troughs with grain.

"In 1525 in Switzerland our ancestors opposed the state church. They believed the teaching of Jesus in the Bible should be practised in small communities where people could help one another and not in a big church run by the state. They didn't believe in baptizing babies either. Baptism was a decision for an adult."

43

Jonah stopped talking to hang a lantern on the post above him, for it was still dark inside the barn.

"So our people were called Anabaptists at first. The rulers said they were destroying the church. Our leaders and many of their followers were put to death...."

Aunt Lydia entered the barn noisily swinging a milking stool in one hand and a bucket in the other. She settled herself beside a restless cow and patted her affectionately on the back.

"The story will go on, Ian, when the women don't make such a noise," Jonah chuckled.

"Bessie is the best cow of all," Aunt Lydia told Ian. "She's Ezra and Susie's favourite. Sometime I'll let you milk her, Ian."

"I don't know how!" Ian exclaimed with alarm.

"It's easy." Aunt Lydia briskly settled herself on the milking stool. "I'll teach you in one morning."

Mary and Sarah, carrying old straw hats upside down, nodded shyly at Ian. They gathered eggs from mysterious places, filling the hats. The Gingerich brothers, two bearded men who looked like Jonah but with brown beards instead of white, were pitching manure from the stalls with long-handled pitchforks into a flat wagon that moved on wooden runners.

"See that stone boat with the runners." Reuben pointed to the manure-covered wagon. "Last winter John and I used it for a sled." He stopped abruptly as though the mention of John's name might bring some kind of punishment.

Jonah hobbled up to them. "You take Ian to the loft, Reuben, and throw down the hay and straw. I'll curry the horses this morning."

Reuben frowned.

"Our Reuben has his mind most of the time on horses," Jonah chided. "If you stay with us awhile, Ian, we'll take you to the horse auction in Waterloo. Reuben and his father know something about every horse there."

Reuben blushed. "You will make me proud, Grossdoddy," he said.

"Yah, and that's not good," Jonah admitted.

Ian followed Reuben to an upper level of the barn where the machinery and hay were kept. They walked into it over a gently sloping bank of earth which served as a driveway.

"We Amish have bank barns," Reuben told Ian. "That's the way they were built in Switzerland."

Reuben raced ahead of him into the loft and jumped into a deep pile of straw. Ian joined him. It was soft and springy.

"When we have time on Sunday afternoon, we'll jump into the straw from the rafters," Reuben promised, pointing to the sturdy cross-beams high above them.

They both grabbed pitchforks from hooks on the wall and sent piles of straw sailing through a hole in the floor "to bed down the animals," Reuben said. Then mouthfuls of hay followed to feed the cows and horses. Ian hoped he could remember that straw was for bedding and hay was for eating. What if he got them mixed up?

"They eat oats too." Reuben raced to a bin and filled a bucket with grain. Ian could carry only half as much. They ran to the floor below, filling trough after trough for the horses and cows who munched at it gratefully.

The cows were milked, the animals were fed, the eggs were gathered and the stalls were piled with fresh straw. It was time to wash at the pump and eat Rebecca's steaming breakfast.

Ian was impatient for the silent prayer to end. As soon as it did, he filled his bowl to the top with hot porridge, and after

45

this came eggs, fried potatoes, ham, home-made bread and a dish of preserved cherries.

"Ach, Ian," Jonah smiled, leaning back in a chair and taking Sarah onto his lap. "You have a good appetite. Our people aren't so stylish that we care about getting fat. We just eat until we're full."

"Jonah," Aunt Lydia interrupted. "Tom Higgins was here during chores. The man Turner is better. He's going back home later today." She paused. "He's trying to prove that he didn't cause the accident."

Ian flamed with anger. He couldn't hold back any longer.

"Not guilty of the accident!" he exploded. "How can he say he didn't cause it! I was in that car. He was driving like a lunatic. If you have a lawyer, Jonah, I can tell him the truth. I can tell him what really happened."

"Ach, Ian." Jonah shook his head. He put Sarah down and reached for a big black Bible. "We Amish believe in obeying the law and in telling the truth, but we don't go to a lawyer to settle our problems. The trouble with a lawsuit is that if you lose you lose, and if you win, you lose too — in goodwill."

Ian couldn't believe Jonah meant what he said. He must be joking.

"It's right here in the Bible." Jonah began flipping pages, then read: " 'And if any man sue thee at the law, and take away thy coat, let him have thy cloak also.' And listen to this." Jonah read from another page. " 'Recompense to no man evil for evil ... live peaceably with all men.' "

Ian had read some of the Bible, too, in a required course at his school in London, but he didn't remember these verses. Did these Amish take the Bible literally? Were they all trying to be saints? Or were they just afraid of the law? If Jack Turner was going to tell a big lie and not even offer to pay for the buggy and the dead horse, and if the Benders weren't going to do anything about it, then he would have to help them.

Jonah pulled at his long, white beard. He seemed to be talking now to himself.

"We Amish don't always co-operate. We're not all saintly," he said as though reading Ian's mind. "But I think this Jack Turner will have a guilty conscience until he comes to see Ezra." Jonah paused again and stroked his beard. "We must still try to have forgiveness for one another.... I have to live my own convictions and I'm not one to judge."

Aunt Lydia interrupted again. She spoke more quietly this time.

"Tom Higgins also brought news about Ezra. They are going to operate on his leg. Tomorrow. Susie will stay in the Kitchener hospital with him until it is finished."

The silence in the room was tense. An operation could be serious, Ian realized, and very expensive since the Amish had said they didn't believe in health insurance. The results of the accident were getting worse. Star was dead. Jonah said the smashed buggy could never be repaired, and now there was Ezra's operation. Jack Turner was a coward and a liar and was going back to Chicago because he was afraid to face the Benders. Ian was the only other person in the speeding car. Maybe he would have to take some of the blame.

10

The news of the operation sobered the Bender family. There was so much work on the farm. Jonah was an old man who could hardly walk and John had left the farm or been sent away. The women had to take care of the large farmhouse and the garden and now there was only Reuben left to be the farmer.

A small idea began to grow inside Ian's head. He didn't want to live with Aunt Clem. How could she miss him or be lonely without him? They hardly knew each other.... Dad would be away for the whole winter. He was still bitter that his father had gone without him.... Why couldn't he learn to do some of Ezra's jobs until Ezra got better?

But it wouldn't be easy to live in a place with no electricity and no running water. How could he follow his favourite television programs? What about his record player and tape deck that were being shipped to Aunt Clem's? There was no way to plug it in on the Bender farm. He couldn't have a radio either and he would miss riding in a car. There weren't many books here and no daily paper, no magazines.... But there would be so many new things to learn. He wanted to know as much about horses as Reuben.... Of course, there was still Aunt Clem. She would be trying to call him today. He would just have to tell her that he wasn't coming to Toronto. He wasn't as strong as Reuben, but he would get stronger.... He would ask Jonah about the idea as soon as they were alone.

Today he would show the Benders that he could work. Hadn't Dad told him that some of his Scottish ancestors had chopped down a whole forest along Lake Erie to raise crops and build farm houses?

Jonah approached him. "Ian, you help Reuben today."

Chores continued one after another at a steady pace. The two boys poured sour milk into the pig trough. Scraps of vegetable parings, bits of bread and celery tops floated around on top of it. Ian held his nose.

"They like it," Reuben assured him. "Don't they have pigs where you come from, Ian?" Reuben asked.

"You mean in Chicago?" Ian exclaimed. "Of course not!"

"Well I never heard of that town," Reuben replied. "But I have some cousins in Nottawa, Michigan. Did you ever hear of it?"

"No, I never did," Ian had to admit.

"Then we're even," Reuben laughed.

Ian wondered if the pigs' swelling bodies and rounded cheeks might burst. But they all smiled contentedly. Reuben wasn't worried. He was analysing the baby pigs, who were a pretty pink, unlike their mothers. His father had promised him one to raise on his own, he told Ian. He was going to choose it carefully.

The September sun rose, burnished and warm. It reflected the ripe apples, the red tomatoes, the orange pumpkins, the brown potatoes and the yellow corn.

"The tomatoes need picking," Jonah called to the two boys. They filled basket after basket. Ian's arms ached. His fingers were caked with dirt. His feet were sore. Didn't farmers ever rest? Ian sat down in the soft dirt between a row of tomato plants. Reuben relaxed too. He began to talk about Star.

"We bred him lightweight," he said. "He trotted with his head in the air. His legs were slim and straight. Once he galloped with John and me on his back through the back fields, faster than the wind in a storm. It's a good thing Poppa didn't see us."

"Reuben, what happened to John?" Ian decided to ask. He continued to rest on the soft dirt. He couldn't pick another tomato.

"You wouldn't understand," Reuben answered slowly. "You come from the 'outside'."

"I'll try," Ian promised.

"He bought a car, and the Rules of our church don't allow cars." Reuben became sober and settled himself beside Ian. "He can't be punished by the church because he isn't a member yet. No one can join before they're sixteen and some people like John, who's nineteen, wait longer. But Grossdoddy says John can't come home until he sells the car. Grossdoddy is the Bishop and our family has to set a good example."

"But that's crazy." Ian was amazed that this was all John had done. "Couldn't John keep the car somewhere else?" he prodded.

"Some of the Amish boys buy cars and hide them until they become church members," Reuben confided. "Then they shape up. They are just playing the devil a bit, Grossdoddy told me."

Reuben and he were finally talking together like friends. Ian was pleased. Maybe now he could ask more questions.

"Grossdoddy and Mom and Poppa are afraid John will become like Hannah," Reuben added softly.

"Hannah?" Ian was surprised by another new name.

"Hannah was my sister, but she isn't in our family any more." Reuben's face was expressionless. "She joined the church and then she married an 'Englischer' — that's an 'Outsider'. She went to a university and now she's a nurse in a hospital."

"But what's wrong with that?" Ian protested. "She's still your sister!"

"I guess you don't know what the Bible says." Reuben was serious. " 'Do not be conformed to this world.' Romans 12. When we join the church we have to live separate from the evil world. Hannah left us. She has to be shunned until she repents."

These ideas shocked Ian. He couldn't understand them.

"But she hasn't done anything wrong."

"Grossdoddy says there's no way we can have people in our church who hold different values and not be influenced by them. He says if it doesn't matter how we dress or wear our hair, or whether we ride in buggies or in cars, we can't be a separate people."

There was a long silence between them.

"I still miss her," Reuben admitted, "and Momma cries sometimes when she looks at Hannah's sign."

"What sign?"

"She printed a big sign when she was a little girl. It always hung on her bedroom wall until she left. It said: I WANT TO BE A NURSE. Momma keeps it in her cedar chest."

The story saddened Ian. How could these people be so forgiving to a man like Jack Turner and refuse to see their own daughter and sister? Reuben began picking tomatoes again. But Ian couldn't remain silent.

"Another thing. I still don't see why it's better to ride around the country in horses and buggies, Reuben. I bet that isn't in the Bible."

"You sure ask a lot of questions," Reuben laughed. "I just finished telling you that horses and buggies help us to keep separated from the world." He waited and then added. "I don't like cars. They are the reason for John leaving, and a car killed Star."

The noise of approaching horses and buggies coming up the farm lane ended their conversation.

"Grossdoddy won't like it that we didn't finish the tomatoes," Reuben said as they ran from the garden to the farm house.

Amish men, women and children jumped from their buggies and Reuben ran among them, helping to tie the horses to hitching posts. Ian watched. Everyone spoke Pennsylvania Dutch. They smiled in his direction, seeming to know who he was. Some carried baskets of food. From the back of one of the buggies four men lifted a large copper kettle. They took it to the back of the house and hooked it by a chain to a black metal trivet. A fire was started beneath it with gathered logs.

Ian was completely baffled. What were they doing now?

Women poured kettles of steaming red tomato juice inside and Aunt Lydia added spices. A wooden paddle with a long handle was plunged into the thick, bubbling juice. Jonah sat on a stool nearby and began pushing the handle back and forth, stirring slowly. Reuben and Ian were asked to help line rows and rows of clean bottles on a table. There were hundreds of them.

51

"It's going to be catsup," Reuben finally told Ian.

"Amish catsup," smiled Jacob.

"Can I have a turn stirring?" Ian asked. He sat on Jonah's stool and pushed the wooden handle back and forth rapidly. Juice splashed over the sides of the kettle in all directions.

"Not so fast, Ian." Jonah stood beside him. "Each job has its own set time and it can't be hurried."

Ian slowed down.

I'll bet in a catsup factory, Ian thought to himself, they stir this juice with a big electric mixer and it gets done in half the time. And they probably have a capping machine for these hundreds of bottles.

In the midst of all the strange Pennsylvania Dutch words flowing around him, Ian frequently heard the names Ezra, Susie and Star. The accident must be on the minds of all these people.

"The operation on Ezra is serious," he heard Jonah say in English to his friend Gravy Dan. "The doctor might not be able to save his leg."

Ian was horrified. He hadn't heard this news. It was bad enough for Ezra to smash his leg, but he never dreamt that he might lose it! Why wasn't everyone more alarmed and concerned? But what could he do about it? He continued to stir slowly and the juice got thicker. Smells of spiced tomato juice drifted through the Indian-summer stillness. Aunt Lydia dipped small spoonfuls of it on thin slices of bread for everyone to taste.

Ian smacked his lips. "It does taste better than catsup from the grocery store," he confessed to Jonah.

"Stir it a little longer, Ian," Aunt Lydia directed. "Susie should be here to taste. She is the best one to do this."

Soon Ian walked away from the others and lay down on a patch of tall, green grass. His back ached, the muscles in his arms and legs were unbelievably tired, his bare feet were scratched and bruised, and he was sick at heart about the possible loss of Ezra's leg.

"When will all this work end?" he sighed with wonder that there could be so much to do, for Jonah was now talking about digging up potatoes and ploughing one of the fields.

Mary, barefoot and in her long purple dress, settled close

beside him. Wisps of golden hair which escaped from her tight black cap framed her pretty face. She carried a small, worn book.

"I can read you a poem, Ian," she smiled shyly.

Ian wanted to hug her. He didn't know she had even noticed him. Surely she was too small to read.

"I go to school," she smiled again. "This year I'll be in the second grade."

She began to read,

> "Along the line of smoky hills
> The crimson forest stands
> And all the day the blue jays call
> Throughout the autumn lands.
>
> Now by the brook, the maple leans
> With all her glory spread
> And all the sumac on the hills
> Have turned from green to red."

Mary's words were a lullaby. Ian sank into the grass and fell asleep with one hand touching the sleeve of her old-fashioned dress.

He didn't stir until she yanked his arm.

"You slept a long time, Ian," she said, no longer bashful with him. "You missed your dinner. Grossdoddy says you are a city boy who doesn't know how to work yet. He says you will learn." She handed him a glass of milk and a big slice of bread with sausage and cheese on top of it, which he ate in a hurry.

What did Jonah mean that he didn't know how to work? Ian was angry. He would show him. Being from the city didn't mean that he was lazy. Did these Amish people think they were the only ones who could do anything? He thanked Mary. The smallest girl, Sarah, peeked at him behind her sister's skirt.

"She can't speak English yet," Mary explained. "She won't learn until she goes to school."

"Sometime I'll play with both of you," Ian promised, "but now I have to work." He ran to join Jonah and Reuben who were standing near the barn with other men and boys. He wondered if they would laugh at him for taking a nap in the middle of the day, but they talked soberly in their own language and paid little attention to him.

The parents gathered their children and prepared to leave. Reuben ran to unhitch the horses and buggies and back them into the lane.

"I'll help him." Ian was determined to do his share of the work. He watched Reuben climb into a buggy and reach for the reins and pull them back. Ian climbed into another empty buggy and did the same thing, pulling the reins as hard as he could. The horse turned his head around, trying to look at Ian, and shook his head furiously. Ian pulled the reins tighter. Foam blew from the animal's mouth with a long shuddering sigh. The horse started backwards and then stopped and pushed back sideways. One of the buggy wheels jammed. Ian heard a loud, sharp noise, but he held onto the reins, pulling them tighter and tighter. The horse neighed loudly and reared up onto his hind legs. There was a crack and the buggy shaft split in two.

Within seconds Reuben was beside Ian on the buggy seat. He grabbed the reins from his hands and, swinging a long whip, gave the animal a crack on the back. There was another shuddering sigh as the horse pawed the ground and at last became calm.

Ian's legs and hands shook. He was more frightened than he had been when Jack Turner's car hit Star. Jonah raised his hand to Ian and helped him down from the high buggy seat.

"I just wanted to help," Ian tried to explain.

Jonah answered quietly. "It takes a long time, Ian, to become a good farmer. If you can stay with us for a while, you will learn. But just remember, God looks at our willingness rather than our ability."

Ian was in no mood to understand at the moment what Jonah was telling him. When he thought about it later, it made a good deal of sense.

Right now, he was angry and ashamed that he couldn't manage the horse. If Reuben could do it, he could too.

11

Ian's problems seemed to pile higher and higher into a tottering heap. Always before he could tell them to his Dad; the two of them had worried together about the solutions. But his father was miles away and it might take weeks for letters to travel to and from the Northwest Territories. He had the oil company's phone number, but Dad might not be available. There was no phone at the Benders for Dad to call back and anyway he wasn't yet sure what he wanted to say.

He couldn't ignore Aunt Clem much longer. She was a determined woman. She expected him for the winter and she didn't change plans abruptly. What would she think of this farm where he wanted to stay? "No electricity! No inside bathroom! No rugs! No curtains! No automobile! It's not civilized!..." He could just hear her.

The fantasy of believing he could escape backward in time was totally banished every time he stood on the slope of ground that led to the second floor of the barn. He could see cars in the distance speeding one after another along a busy, modern highway.

Jonah appeared at his side tapping with his cane.

"We're ploughing one of the fields this afternoon for winter wheat, Ian," he said. "Reuben is going to use the one-furrow plough. You walk behind it with him and watch. If you could stay with us for a time, you might be able to help plough the corn fields next month."

"If you could stay with us ..." Ian repeated Jonah's words over and over to himself. Jonah had said it four times now. He must really mean it. Maybe he wasn't joking about learning to plough?

Jonah stood squarely in front of him. His wide chest pulled at the buttons of his homemade shirt with each deep breath, and the flowing white beard moved up and down. Jonah's sharp blue eyes, half closed with tiredness, looked directly into Ian's. There was a mixture of laughter and approval in them.

"I can see you don't give up easily, Ian," he said.

"I'll find Reuben right away." Ian ran through the large barn door to the stalls where Reuben was throwing a harness over a huge dapple gray horse.

"Hi, Reuben." Ian was breathless. "Jonah said you'd show me how to plough and how to harness a horse."

"Sure, Ian." Reuben smoothed the horse's sides with both hands. "Dick here is a Percheron Gelding. See his big strong feet and look how broad he is across the chest. I like him best, next to Star. He has an honest face and he'll do anything for Poppa and me."

Reuben put his thumb into the side of big Dick's mouth, slipping a steel bit into an open space between his teeth. Ian shuddered. Could he do this? Wouldn't the horse bite with those sharp, white teeth? Then Ian looked at Dick's gentle, placid brown eyes. If Reuben could stick his finger inside Dick's mouth, he could too.

"Help me get the bridle behind his ears," Reuben said. Ian slipped the leather strap behind the two stiff, pointed ears.

"Giddyup," Reuben called out to Dick.

"Giddyup," Ian shouted as loudly as he could.

The horse backed up obediently from his stall.

Outside, Dick was hooked up to a small plough. Reuben grabbed both handles and also held a single line from the horse in his right hand.

"If I yell "Gee", he'll go right. If I yell "Haw", he goes left," Reuben explained. "Now watch, Ian, I have to plough a straight furrow." Reuben pointed across the huge flat field in front of them. "I keep my eye on that white cloth tied to the fence way over there. It keeps me going straight."

Reuben flicked the line. Dick strained forward with his wide shoulders. The plough cut into the black earth, folding it back in ripples. On the far side of the same field another farmer ploughed with a five-horse hitch. The strong animals bent their heads together as though marching to beating drums in a parade. Their flowing manes streamed out like flags in the wind.

"When you see any rocks, Ian, throw them in a pile between the furrows," Reuben called loudly.

The stones spilled out round and hard from the upturned

soil. Ian hoped he could do this rock-throwing job. It took a lot of strength.

After an exhausting half hour, Jonah hobbled to Ian's side and both of them watched a beardless farmer across the road bouncing comfortably on the seat of a new red tractor. He ploughed swiftly over his fields, taking half the time of the horse-drawn ploughs.

"Why don't you have a tractor?" Ian asked somewhat enviously.

"Yah well," Jonah said. "If people let all these new contraptions do their work for them, they won't have enough work to keep them busy and safe from trouble. And besides," the old man went on with a chuckle in his voice, "a horse reproduces; a tractor produces nothing but debts."

Ian wasn't convinced. "That doesn't sound like a good enough reason."

"Yah well," Jonah went on, "our neighbour across the road does things differently. He plants just one crop to make money and his soil wears out growing the same thing year after year — even with chemical fertilizer. What we do is rotate our crops and plough manure from our own barn into the soil. That way the land is enriched and more can be raised on less land."

Jonah left to go back to the barn as Reuben came towards them, swinging the plough into an arc at the end of another row.

"My turn," said Ian, grabbing the handles of the plough away from Reuben in his eagerness. Reuben hesitated. "Giddyup," Ian cried, wanting to speed up the ploughing and not be totally outstripped by the racing tractor. Dick gave a quick tug and the blades of the hand-plough left the furrow and bounced along over the surface of the field. Dick changed his course and headed for the bush and a lush patch of tall green grass. Ian clung to the handles with all of his strength. The great horse raised his head and shook it free of the restraining line. Then he peacefully lowered his mouth and began to nibble. Ian was sure that he saw a grin on Dick's face.

"Now, what did I do wrong?" Ian stomped up to the animal, his face crimson with indignation. The horse looked at him with feigned innocence.

Reuben bent over laughing. "You look like your head is on

57

fire. You want to learn everything too fast, Ian. Dick doesn't know you and I still have to show you how to hold the handles."

Ian sank to the ground beside Dick. Couldn't he ever do one of these jobs right? His arms ached, his feet hurt and sprays of pain shot through his back each time he bent it. How could he help the Benders if he blundered around like this?

Ian stretched out on the green grass. Dick's sharp, white teeth chomped beside him. He was surprised to discover that he wasn't afraid. He was determined that he and Dick were going to learn to work together. You couldn't feel this way about a tractor, and he'd have to admit this to Jonah.

For the next hour, however, he left the ploughing to Reuben, and consoled himself by piling up as many stones as he could. Eventually Rebecca appeared swinging a bucket of cold lemonade and some tin cups.

"Thirsty, Ian?" she asked and handed him one of the cups. He drank it in two swallows. Rebecca smiled at him warmly.

Reuben ploughed one last furrow before they started back to the barn. As they neared it, Ian saw the back of a police car disappearing down the lane. Grossdoddy Jonah stood in a swirl of dust behind it.

"We've finished," Reuben called out and walked off alone to unharness Dick in the barn. A little spiral of fear uncoiled inside Ian, for Jonah seemed to hesitate on the lane as though wanting to postpone his return to the farmhouse. He leaned so

heavily on his cane that the end of it tunnelled into the ground. The clear blue of his eyes seemed clouded. A hazy glow of amber spread behind Jonah from the setting sun, like the dying embers of a campfire. The muted light illuminated his beard and his white bobbed hair, so that they became startling puffs of luminous clouds. He didn't seem real.

"Ach, Ian." Jonah broke the spell of Indian summer. "The news is not good about Ezra. The leg had to come off in the operation. He must stay in the hospital for some time. The other leg is partially paralysed. He may never walk again."

Ian stood in mute shock. What would the Benders do? How could a man who might never walk again work on an Amish farm? Ian would *have* to stay and help the family now, even with all the blunders he made. And where was John? If he knew about his father, surely John would sell his car and come home? But if John didn't come back, even Aunt Clem might see why Ian had to stay. He forced himself to ask Jonah about her.

"Ach yah, I forgot." Jonah straightened his back and began walking to the farmhouse. Ian saw the shaft he had cracked leaning in two pieces against the barn. It was an embarrassment just to look at them. Jonah didn't notice.

"Your aunt is better," Jonah said. "She is coming for you soon. She doesn't like it that you are staying on an Amish farm."

12

The supper that Aunt Lydia and Rebecca prepared that evening was hardly touched. Even Ian was not hungry. The family were more silent than usual. Tears rolled down the cheeks of little Mary and Sarah. Reuben choked once and had to leave the table. Neighbours came up the farm lane in their buggies and appeared at the kitchen door to inquire and to offer help.

Gravy Dan did all the evening chores and chopped wood for the kitchen stove. Jonah gathered the family in a circle of chairs after dinner for worship and to pray for Ezra.

59

"It is God's will," Jonah ended the service in English. "We are thankful that Ezra is alive."

But the pervasive sadness about Ezra did not interrupt the household schedule. Aunt Lydia bustled about the stove, heating kettles and pots of water. She explained to Ian that it was Saturday night and that one by one everyone would take a bath in the curtained-off room just off the kitchen.

"We must be clean for Sunday," she announced, leaving no opening for anyone to object.

Ian hadn't looked inside the little room before. There was a long, white bathtub along the wall with a drain but no faucet. It would have to be filled over and over again with kettles of water from the stove.

"Why is the bathtub like that?" Ian asked bluntly. "It's a lot more work than having water run into the tub through a pipe."

Aunt Lydia answered simply in her matter-of-fact way.

"If we had electric or telephone wires, or gas or water or sewage lines," she said, "we would tie our house to the outside world."

At family worship Ian had already met the Bible verse about being separate: "Be ye not unequally yoked together with unbelievers." But wasn't the "world" full of both believers and unbelievers, Ian wondered. Perhaps it was harder than it seemed for the Amish to separate themselves, harder than it seemed to practise in everyday life what they believed in church.

Mary and Sarah came first for their baths, then Reuben and Rebecca and Aunt Lydia. Jonah and Ian waited in the kitchen. The old man sat quietly in the rocker beside the stove.

"Jonah." Ian startled him. "Can I spend the winter on your farm if I work hard every day and try to be patient about learning? Would it be a help with the farm work if I stayed?"

Jonah smiled kindly. "Yah well, you could make a good farmer in time, and we surely need extra help." He paused thoughtfully. "But I think you must do what your father and your aunt want. They are your family."

That will be for me to decide, Ian thought to himself. All he needed to know was that Jonah needed him. Tomorrow he would call Aunt Clem from the public telephone down the lane and tell her he wasn't coming to Toronto. He would get

Dad's exact address from her and write a letter at once telling him everything. His father would understand.

All the aching tiredness from the day's work that had left Ian when he heard about the amputation returned in the hot water of his bath.

"Scrub your feet good," Aunt Lydia called to him through the curtain, "and wash your hair."

She sounded like Dad. Didn't they realize he was old enough to know how to take a bath. He pulled the plug for the water to run out and then put on the nightshirt Aunt Lydia had laid out for him and crept quietly up the stairs. He slid into his side of the warm bed. Then he saw Reuben standing in his nightshirt looking out the open window. Reuben could touch the branches of a nearby maple tree. His shoulders shook, but he made no sound. Ian knew that he was crying because of his father. Ian was silent. He too would cry, and not want anyone to see, if his Dad had lost a leg and might never walk again. Ian turned down the lamp wick and blew out the flame.

The only sound in the sleeping Bender household was the ticking clock in the kitchen. It was the middle of the night, however, when a strange sound interrupted both Ian's sleep and the ticking of the clock. Ian stirred. Was he dreaming? He tried to wake but his eyes wouldn't open. Far away, in the back of his head, he heard the scraping sound of steel buggy wheels and the trot of a single horse.

A light flashed over Ian's eyes. He tried brushing it away. It flashed again. Reuben began squirming around on his side of the bed. The light flashed over Reuben. This time both of them sat up. Reuben scrambled out of bed and tiptoed to the window.

"Elam is here. He's come to see Becky!" Reuben whispered excitedly. Ian tiptoed beside him. He could see a horse and buggy tied to the shed and a young man in a white shirt and a broad black hat blinking a flashlight off and on over the bedroom windows.

Reuben began pulling on his clothes. Ian decided he should too.

"We'll have to wait until Becky goes downstairs and lets him in the kitchen, then we'll have some fun."

61

"Fun?" Ian wondered if he had heard the wrong word.

"Elam has a new courting buggy. He's been taking Rebecca home from the Sunday evening singings." Reuben was getting so excited that he forgot to whisper. "It's supposed to be a secret that they are seeing each other," Reuben chuckled.

The boys stopped talking. Quiet footsteps could be heard going down the stairs. The kitchen door squeaked open.

"Come on, Ian, we'll climb down the maple tree." Reuben scrambled over the window sill, grabbed a branch and swung towards the trunk of the sturdy tree. Ian gasped. Could he do that too? He hugged a large branch and dropped from the window ledge. For a frightening second he hung in space, then his feet touched another wide branch below. He stood still to calm the crazy beating of his heart.

Reuben was already on the ground, motioning for him to hurry. He climbed down as fast as he could, stepping from limb to limb with painstaking sureness. He'd never been in a tree before.

"We'll play a trick on them," Reuben laughed. "We'll take off one of the buggy wheels and hang it by a rope way up high in the maple tree."

First they gave Elam's horse a bag full of oats to keep her quiet. Then Ian held the wheel while Reuben quietly unfastened it. The spokes gleamed with fresh black paint in the pale moonlight. They rolled the wheel to the tree and Reuben quickly untied a rope from Mary and Sarah's swing that hung on the lowest branch.

"I'll climb up with the rope, then I'll let it down so you can tie on the wheel, Ian." Reuben was whispering again because they were near the house.

Ian watched as Reuben climbed to the edge of a high branch, pulling the black buggy wheel slowly upwards through the branches. Soon it hung alone, strangely abandoned and looking as if it had dropped from some riderless carriage in the sky.

"Come on up, Ian," Reuben called from the bedroom window.

Ian propped a board against the tree trunk to give him an easier grasp on the lowest branch. He pulled himself painfully up from branch to branch. His arms were scratched and the palms of his hands felt raw. Reuben reached out the window and gave him a hand onto the ledge.

"We can see the wheel from the bed, Ian. We'll watch and see how Elam gets it down." Reuben folded his clothes neatly over a chair and jumped under the blankets. Ian did the same.

"I know what we can do," Ian said, now fully caught up in the conspiracy. "Let's put a sheet over us and scare Elam when he climbs up the tree."

Reuben giggled — but within minutes they were both fast asleep.

13

Sloshing rain had come in the night, washing away the colours and magic of autumn. There was the unwelcome feel of early winter, as though icicle fingers had pried under the cracks of the door and windows.

But chores didn't end for rain, or cold, or Sunday, Ian discovered. It was still dark outside when Aunt Lydia called them to get up. Even before opening his eyes, Ian had smelt a clammy dampness in the air. He expected the fog to float through the open window, thick and in billows. But he didn't want it to swallow him this time. He wanted to be free of it.

Then he remembered the buggy wheel and laughed. All sense of impending danger snapped and when he looked at the limb of the maple tree it was empty. Reuben sat beside him. They winked at one another.

Outside there was a sense of hurry about the chores. They raced together to the end of the lane where a sign swung from two posts announcing:

Vegetables and Fruit
Jonah Bender's Farm
No Sunday Sales

With black crayon, they underlined the last line, so no-one would stop for fresh fruits and vegetables on this day of rest.

Ian went alone to the loft to throw down hay and straw to

63

the animals. He hung the pitchfork with special care over its hook on the barn wall. Reuben let him comb all of one side of big Dick's back with the curry comb.

"Church is at the Zehr farm today," Reuben told Ian. "It's five miles down the road. We'll have to hurry to get there on time."

Ian already knew that the Amish held their church in the homes and barns of their members, believing that "The Lord of Heaven dwelleth not in temples ..." He found it hard to imagine turning a house or barn into a church, but the Amish were full of surprises. Ian thought fleetingly of the towering gray-stone Presbyterian church in Chicago that he and Dad had sometimes attended. The plain Amish would never fit in such a place.

There was a special quiet about the farm this morning. Was it always this way on Sunday or was it because of Ezra? The wet fog and some light drizzle persisted, drumming at Ian's unease. Inside the farmhouse it was quiet too. But there was a polishing of faces, hair, hands and clothing that Ian liked. Jonah stood alone on the porch, his long black Sunday coat with split tails and white starched shirt underneath giving him a solemn and impressive look. He looked older and more bent, as though Ezra's amputation had taken away a part of Jonah too.

"Grossdoddy will preach this morning," Reuben whispered as he stood with Ian near the kitchen stove. "He became a preacher thirty years ago, and later he became a bishop."

After breakfast, Ian and Reuben changed into clean clothes. Inside the kitchen Mary and Sarah stood patiently in bright blue dresses and aprons while Aunt Lydia brushed out their long gold-brown hair. Ian watched admiringly. With flying fingers Lydia made straight partings down the middle of their heads, twisting the hair on either side back tightly and making pig-tail braids behind. She secured all of it beneath their black caps.

"Now you don't look so 'stroobly'." She brushed them aside to help Rebecca with breakfast.

"See my new shoes, Ian." Mary stuck a sturdy black shoe in front of him with a black stocking tucked inside. "They were brown when we got them at the shoe-store sale. Then Poppa

64

dyed them black." She spoke a little sadly, then brightened. "Someday I want my hair to get red like yours."

Aunt Lydia laughed. "If God had wanted you to have red hair, Mary, He would have made it that way. Ian probably has a red-headed father."

Ian frowned. It hurt to be reminded of Dad. He was trying not to think about him too much. Yet a dozen times a day he thought of questions he wanted to ask him. He wanted to show him big Dick and old Bessie, whom he was learning to milk. He wanted him to meet this family. But most of all, he still wanted to be in the Northwest Territories.

Rebecca's Sunday dress was black with a white apron. She bent over the steaming porridge, greeting no-one.

"She didn't get much sleep last night," Reuben whispered in Ian's ear. Rebecca was so beautiful, Ian thought, that if he were a painter he would put her in a frame. But, of course, Rebecca would have none of this. The Amish wouldn't even allow photographs — something to do with worshipping a "graven image".

Aunt Lydia interrupted briskly.

"Here's your jacket, Ian, with the zipper fixed." She shook the newly cleaned and mended jacket and handed it to Ian. "We don't wear zippers on our clothes. It's the first time I've had a good look at one." Jonah came from the porch to join them and bent over the jacket to examine it.

"Ach well," he shrugged his shoulders. "I hear they get stuck a lot and aren't much good." Jonah appeared tireder than usual. Worry had deepened the wrinkles that lined his face.

Upstairs Ian found a white shirt and sombre black pants laid out for him. There was also a pair of heavy black shoes. Once again he rebelled. Dressing like an Amishman for farm work was one thing, but he didn't have to go to church and wear this stiff Sunday outfit.

"I'm not going," Ian said abruptly.

Reuben was puzzled. "Are you feeling sick, Ian? I want to show you the creek on the Zehr farm where we fish ... and in the afternoon after church we can play chess on the Zehrs' home-made set ... and —" Reuben blushed "— I want you to meet Amanda Zehr. She's pretty."

Ian grew more interested. He hesitated, then slowly put on

the black pants and the shoes with their high tops and clomped down the stairs. The two-seated buggy was waiting in the farmyard. Jonah was the driver with Aunt Lydia and the two girls in front. Ian, Reuben and Rebecca sat behind them.

Most of the fog had evaporated and now the air sparkled with sunshine. Prince trotted briskly down the lane. When they came to the main road, other buggies turned from their own lanes to join them until there was a long row of buggies, vividly black against a clearing blue sky. Their occupants were all dressed alike and looked just like their ancestors of almost 300 years ago. Reuben constantly whispered into Ian's ear about each horse — its good points and its bad ones, the kind it was, its age, how much it had cost at the auction.

"You know the horses better than the people, Reuben." Reuben nodded shrewdly.

Not everyone came to the Zehr farm by buggy. Those who lived nearby walked down the smooth dirt road through the morning sunlight that filtered between rows of golden maple boughs. Ian watched them in their long black dresses and white aprons, their white shirts and black-tailed coats.

In the Zehr farmyard, which seemed to have been trimmed for the occasion, the horses and buggies were tied to hitching rails, and as the kitchen clock struck nine everyone walked inside the house. Ian had no idea what to expect. Jonah, the Bishop, with a solemn-looking deacon and two ministers, sat in a centre row of chairs between the kitchen and the living-room. They kissed each other on the cheek. Backless benches filled the rooms. All other furniture had been moved upstairs and partitions had been taken down. The floors and windows had all been scrubbed and polished.

Each age-group walked in together and found their places — the women, girls and babies in one room and the men and boys in the other, a hundred people all told. Ian sat on a bench beside Reuben. The slow, mournful tones of a hymn began with Rebecca's Elam setting the pitch and singing the first word of each line. There was no accompaniment. Ian looked in the hymn book. The words were in German and the date above most of the verses was 1534. He could never sing such slow tunes that seemed weighted with sadness.

A young preacher stood and began speaking in German, the language they used for preaching and for prayer. Children folded handkerchieves into mice and rabbits. Babies were carried upstairs to be nursed. Ian counted the ears of everyone in front of him. He shoved his feet back and forth inside the heavy shoes and lifted each finger up and down, fearful that they might stop moving.

Thirty minutes ticked away before the preacher sat down. Another slow hymn began. The room got warm. Ian's eyelids drooped. His head fell on Reuben's shoulder and both boys dozed. When they woke, Jonah was preaching in German and the older people were listening intently.

Ian watched Jonah's face grow serious, sad and then peaceful. What was he saying that could go on for an hour? He'd have to learn this language. He might as well be deaf without it. Aunt Lydia was a teacher. He would ask her to help. Ian glanced at the bobbing heads of many children around him and fixed his eyes on the kitchen clock as a third interminable hour ticked by. He squirmed and twisted on the backless bench. How could Reuben and the other boys and girls endure this every other week?

Eventually Jonah stopped talking. Everyone turned and knelt over the benches for silent prayer. The service was over. Reuben and Ian bounded out the door and into the welcoming sunshine.

"Yippeeeeee!" Ian cried, flinging out his arms in joyous release from their long imprisonment. Reuben stopped and looked at him aghast. Ian suddenly remembered Jonah saying

67

that on Sundays all Amish farms are quiet. Not even a hammer pounds or a plough creaks over the ground.

Inside the house there was quiet chatting as all the benches were turned upside down to make tables for lunch. When it was Ian and Reuben's turn, they spread bread with a home-made mixture of peanut butter and maple syrup. The delicious taste made all the waiting seem worthwhile.

Amanda Zehr poured apple cider from a pitcher for Ian and Reuben. Her round, rosy face was the image of an apple. Reuben blushed again.

"She's not that pretty," Ian thought and dipped his spoon into the peanut butter jar for more spread.

The lazy afternoon was happy, though Ezra's operation ran like a black thread through all the talk and all the play. There were strolls along the creek by joking boys who told of fish they had caught and were going to catch. A home-made chess board was unearthed from a kitchen cupboard and Ian found that Reuben was his match.

When mid-afternoon came, most of the buggies left for home and the waiting chores, but the young men and women gathered in the Zehrs' large barn for games and singing. Ian and Reuben were too young to join in, but Rebecca wasn't. She would come home much later in Elam's courting buggy.

As the Benders entered their own land, they saw a car parked in the farmyard.

"It must be Tom Higgins with more news about Ezra." Jonah drew in the reins and stepped down from the buggy, fastening it for the moment to a hitching post. The others followed him.

The car was sleek and black with a silver trim around the middle and bore no resemblance to the policeman's automobile. A husky-looking man, wearing a cap with a small peak, hunched over the steering wheel. Sitting behind him and leaning forward was a stocky, middle-aged woman. She was smartly dressed in a black wool suit with a matching hat that tilted forward over one eye.

"I don't know them," Jonah said.

The car stopped and the man stepped out. His shoulders remained hunched as though he were still bending over his steering-wheel.

"Clementine McDonald has come for her nephew, Ian." He was addressing Jonah and bowed a little forward.

Ian stared at him but didn't move.

"Tell the lady to come inside," Jonah offered.

The driver returned to the car and spoke to Ian's aunt in low tones. She handed him an envelope, but didn't move.

"Mrs. McDonald isn't well yet," the driver said. He gave the envelope to Jonah. "This is to pay for Ian's expenses while he has been your guest."

The driver turned suddenly to Ian, saying "Come along, now." He seemed embarrassed and eager to leave. "Your Aunt said all your clothes were lost in the accident, so you don't have any baggage."

Ian ignored him, walked quickly to the car and faced his aunt.

"Hello, Aunt Clem," he said hesitantly, noticing that she didn't look ill. "I was going to call you on the telephone today. I've decided not to come to Toronto. I'm going to stay here on the farm."

"Oh!" Aunt Clem exclaimed, bending forward and looking at him closely through the bifocal part of her glasses. Ian noticed that her double chin was fatter than the last time he saw her. "We'll talk about this going back to Toronto. Now get inside the car, Ian. The damp air isn't good for me."

Ian took a step backward.

"I'm not coming, Aunt Clem," he said firmly. "I'm going to stay here and help the Benders."

"Ernest." Ian heard his aunt speak to her driver. "Bring the boy to the car."

Ian felt himself being pulled to the car by a strong grip around his arm. He pulled back and dug his feet into the ground, but it was no use. He was pushed into the back seat beside his aunt and the door was closed.

14

The smooth-running car easily spun a circle in the farmyard and headed for the open road. The Bender family were nothing more than a blue-coloured blur. Ian couldn't even wave goodbye.

He had known Aunt Clem might come to the farm for him, but he didn't think she would swoop down like a hawk and pluck him off the ground. He *couldn't* just let place after place be chopped out of his life. He would probably never see Tony in Chicago again. Now this departure was even worse. He hadn't thanked the Benders or told them how sorry he was about the accident.

The lump in his throat was there again. In a rush of frustration, he realized that the Amish family had become a real home for him. He knew now why he wanted to stay with them. It wasn't just because he felt guilty about the accident. He *liked* them. And they gave him a special place at their table. He couldn't agree with them on their separation from the world and their refusal to use lawyers, and he wouldn't kneel on the floor with them at family worship, but he had already started to say his own silent prayers when they did. Reuben said he seemed like a brother. Mary had read him a poem and leaned her head against his shoulder. He even wanted to call Jonah Grandad — he'd never known his own grandparents.

Ian held his thoughts inside him and looked out the window. A strange sight flashed by — an old blue car driven by a young boy pulling an Amish buggy behind it as though it were a piece of junk. Ian felt miserable as it vanished into the distance. So far Aunt Clem had said nothing. He was glad. It was a jolt to return to the twentieth century and see car after car whizzing by. Even a few days in the seventeenth century had slowed his pace and adjusted his eyes to a different way of living.

At last Aunt Clem turned to him, looking over the top of her glasses like a police inspector.

"Those clothes you are wearing look ridiculous," she said as the car swung onto the 401 highway and headed for Toronto. Ian was still wearing the home-made pants and the button-on suspenders. "I've seen pictures of Amish people in the newspapers. They seem very inflexible and backward. Are they able to read and write?"

Ian didn't respond. Such a stupid question didn't deserve an answer.

"You'll have to have some new clothes at once," said Aunt Clem, looking him over carefully. "I'm not going to walk into a store with you looking the way you do. I'll call Eaton's tomorrow and have them send some suitable things to the house in your size."

Ian felt sick. Aunt Clem was condemning his new friends, and he didn't know how to talk to her. He made up his mind not to.

Aunt Clem's house in Toronto had a trim, solid look. A row of angular hedges boxed in the front lawn, and one clipped evergreen stood near the front entrance. The grass around the house was so evenly cut it had the appearance of a rug. Ian's eyes travelled to the one untrimmed, wild-flung object of beauty in the yard. A maple tree at the side of the house glowed with a mass of golden leaves that spread in all directions. Looking at it, Ian vividly remembered climbing the tree beside the window at the Bender farm.

Aunt Clem pulled the heavy front door open with a ponderous swing and a waft of linseed-oil furniture polish greeted them. Her dark, shiny antique furniture filled all the rooms. The pieces didn't "take to the light", so heavy velvet curtains held the sun at bay.

The chair in the living-room that Ian usually sat in had carved legs with claw-and-ball feet. Once as a small boy he had been certain he saw the wooden talons spread out and begin to walk. He had sat rigid with fright, until Aunt Clem had scoffed at his fears.

"I'm sorry our first day together had such a bad beginning, Ian." Aunt Clem's lips pursed around a long pin which she pulled from the back of her hat. "The accident must have been a shock for you. I couldn't call your father about it. He phoned on Friday and gave me his number, then went straight out to an oil rig. He may be back tomorrow, but he wasn't sure, so why don't we both write him a letter? I've addressed an envelope to him and put it in your room."

She hung her hat carefully on an imposing oak hall-stand. Ian decided that perhaps he should answer her — maybe she really wanted to know what happened after all — but she didn't give him a chance.

"I don't understand your wanting to stay on that farm, Ian. I guess you didn't know what you were doing. And those clothes —" she began to laugh "— I know they're not your doing, but they do look preposterous."

Ian felt his face go red. It was embarrassing to be talked to like this. Didn't Aunt Clem realize what had happened? She sent him off to wash his hands, instructing him to appear in the dining-room shortly. An elderly woman cook presided at all times in the kitchen, even though she might be serving only Aunt Clem. She also brought the food to the table.

Ian wasn't hungry. He picked at the dishes placed in front of him and wondered what Rebecca and Aunt Lydia were serving at the farm. Who would help Reuben with his chores? This was the day they had planned to jump off the barn rafters into the straw. Without thinking Ian took a slice of bread, buttered it, and began wiping his plate clean with it.

Aunt Clem's knife and fork clattered onto her plate.

"Well!" She cleared her throat, staring with a mixture of shock and dismay. "I suppose those Amish taught you that."

Ian said nothing.

"Ian McDonald." Aunt Clem was exasperated. "You haven't said one word since you got into the car. Now explain about that bread!"

Ian looked down at his plate, dropping the bread on the tablecloth. What could he say? Wiping his plate with a piece of bread had seemed to make sense on the farm.

Aunt Clem patted her lips carefully with her white linen napkin, then laid it properly beside her plate. She cleared her throat.

"If you aren't going to talk, Ian, then I will have to talk to you. The first thing we will discuss is the accident."

Ian's heart started to pound.

"That nice man, Jack Turner, called me just before he left the hospital to go back to Chicago," Aunt Clem said in her polite, firm way. "He told me about the great hazard of having those slow-moving buggies on the highways. Something should be done about them. I don't understand why those people must drive around in horses and buggies in the twentieth century. I'm afraid Mr. Turner is entirely right to plead innocent."

This was enough! Maybe Dad was right about the tempers of red-headed Scotsmen constantly boiling under their skin.

"You better not talk that way about the Benders," Ian said loudly, his face flaming. "Jack Turner is a liar. He was driving over seventy miles an hour before he hit their buggy. The Benders were not on a highway. They were on a country road. The buggy was travelling on the shoulder of the road where it was supposed to be." Ian's voice shook. "Jack Turner killed their horse. He caused Ezra Bender to have his leg cut off and be disabled for the rest of his life. He's a liar and a murderer!"

"Well!" Aunt Clem leaned back in her chair to survey her nephew. Her black eyes snapped.

"I suppose now you're going to tell me you want to become one of those Amishmen?" Her question had a sinister note.

"Yes." Ian continued to speak loudly. "I want to become one of those Amishmen." The idea had never entered his head until this moment.

Aunt Clem was quiet. She closed her eyes for a moment to collect her thoughts. When she half opened them she appeared to be peering into the distance as though Ian was far beneath her.

"Ian McDonald." She rose from her chair. "This is enough. I will not have you talk to me in a disorderly and uncouth manner. You will go up to your room without dessert. You will stay there until you are ready to apologize."

Ian banged his napkin on the table and strode swiftly up the stairs to the bedroom he already knew was his. He opened the door, grateful to find that the bolt was still on the inside of it. He slid it into place at once. The room hadn't changed. Thick, menacing pieces of black furniture stood there

73

defiantly. The white walls hadn't a pin-prick on them. If the furniture too had been white, it could have been a hospital room.

In a neat pile on the desk were envelopes, paper and a pen. Good, Ian thought. He would write to his father at once and tell him exactly what had happened and why he must leave Aunt Clem's house. After that he would write to the Benders and tell them he was coming back to help as soon as he could contact his Dad.

Ian was still furious. How could his aunt believe someone like Jack Turner whom she didn't know? And where did she get her ideas about the Amish? She was treating him like a five-year-old.

He smoothed the paper flat on the desk. Words tumbled onto the page. He relived each moment of the accident. He could almost see Dad sitting in front of him listening. He might not agree with him, but at least he would believe him.

At the end of the letter he wrote:

Dad, I feel horribly guilty. I feel like I helped cause all the suffering, maybe because Jack Turner ran away.

I have to go back to the farm. They need me there and Aunt Clem doesn't. Please call her at once. I don't know how to talk to her. I miss you.

Ian

P.S. I don't really understand why the Amish want to work so hard and live like pioneers. But I bet those McDonalds who came to Canada from Scotland and chopped down pine trees along Lake Erie to build their homes lived pretty much like the Amish do today.

Ian stuffed the pages of the letter in the envelope and sealed it. He would mail it somehow early tomorrow morning. But even then it might take a week before Dad would get it in the Northwest Territories. A week was a long time to be away from the farm. Maybe he could convince Aunt Clem that he should go back there for a visit. He had two $10 bills in his jacket pocket. He could buy a ticket on the bus or train.

It was getting dark. Ian tugged at the heavy drapes to pull

74

them back. A bountiful array of colours flooded the room. Beside his window was the tall maple tree flaming with golden leaves. Ian pushed the window open quietly. The screen was loose so he unhooked it and pulled it inside.

He touched the leaves. This tree was closer to the house than the one at the farm. He remembered the buggy wheel hanging in the top of the Benders' tree and laughed. Aunt Clem's tree had bigger limbs, too. It would be easy to climb down ... climb down.... Of course. He could do it!

15

The idea hit Ian like an explosion. He would climb down the tree when it got dark and make his way to the farm. He had Dad's phone number now, written on a slip of paper on his desk. He would call him when he got there so he wouldn't worry. He would leave a note for Aunt Clem which she would find in the morning. It was the only way to tell her why he couldn't live with her.

Aunt Clem went to bed early and her room was across the hall. She couldn't see him from her window. The $20 was safe in his jacket pocket. He could easily take the subway from Aunt Clem's to Union Station — he had often done it with Dad — buy a train ticket to Kitchener, and then hitch-hike to Milltown. Jonah's farm was only two miles from there.

He looked at his baggy Amish pants. They would attract attention. Maybe he'd left some clothes last Christmas. He searched in the dresser drawers — then in the closet. Far at the back on a hanger were a pair of blue corduroys. They had been too big last year and Dad had said to leave them. Ian quickly tried them on. They just fit.

The excitement of leaving was mixed with some fear. What if he fell from the tree? What if Aunt Clem caught him before he left? She couldn't tolerate disobedience. He could imagine her putting bars across his bedroom window. In movies and books escapes were planned carefully; every detail was mastered in advance.

Ian decided he would roll up the Amish pants into a bundle and tie them with the suspenders around his waist. He would need them when he got back to the farm. He would wear the jacket with the money and Dad's address and phone number safely zipped in the inside pocket.

"I better study the tree before it gets completely dark," he thought. "I need to know where the big branches are and which one I'm going to swing onto."

He wrote Aunt Clem's note carefully and put it in the middle of his desk. She couldn't miss seeing it. He drew a small skull and crossbones in the corner just to give her something to think about. He decided to keep the door bolted and to leave the desk light on so Aunt Clem would think he was in the room.

His planning was cut off quickly for Aunt Clem's firm footsteps could be heard coming up the stairs. She stopped outside Ian's door.

"Ian." She raised her voice as though the door were made of five feet of cement. "Are you ready to apologize yet?"

Ian started to shout back, feeling just as angry with her as before. But for some reason he thought of Jonah and how he had said one morning at breakfast, "I try the best I can to live peaceably with all men." In a normal but firm voice Ian answered, "No, I'm not ready to apologize yet."

Aunt Clem's feet stomped away.

At last it was dark and time for Ian to grab the tree limb and jump. He took a breath so deep it was like drinking in the wind. Then with both hands he grasped the tree limb and pushed himself headlong into the dark. The limb bent lower and lower, bouncing and waving him up and down — teasing him like a swing. He wondered if he could hang on, for his hands were slipping from their grip. Then his feet touched a sturdy limb and he climbed down carefully, one branch after another. He jumped to the ground and stood, wobbly and uncertain. His arms felt as though they had been stretched from their moorings.

He looked cautiously upward. Surely all the noise he'd made swinging about in the tree limbs had disturbed Aunt Clem? But all he could see was one of the drapes flapping from the open window, waving an eerie goodbye.

He hurried along several streets towards the dark, tunnelled subway. It could have been a snake hole without any end, for there were no other people and no other sounds but the click of his coins in the box at the turnstile.

It was still Sunday, almost a holiday for the subway. When Ian stepped into a car it rattled with emptiness. He welcomed the noise and clamour of some children who boarded with roller skates dangling from their shoulders. Ian remembered roller skating with Dad in Calgary in a sweeping arena that spun them around and around.

"UNION STATION" appeared on the wall of the subway before he expected it. The cavernous railroad station which he remembered as busy and swollen with crowds was like a calm ocean today. It swallowed the few ant-like people, such as Ian, who spilled from its underground rivulets. Would he ever get to the far-away ticket counter? When he did reach up to the window and ask for "A one-way ticket to Kitchener, please", his voice was hollow and sounded like forced air blowing through an empty tube.

Luckily a train was due to leave in twenty minutes. The train car was virtually empty and a conductor at the back of it opened one sleepy eye as Ian entered. Ian sat behind two elderly women, the only other passengers in the compartment, who jabbered intently into each other's faces. Their white hair was filled with silver bobby pins that slipped down their necks. They didn't notice Ian. He wished they might be like the elderly ladies in Holland who, when he and Dad happened to ride in a train compartment with them, had smiled and shared their box lunch.

When the train started, Ian relaxed for the first time since being snatched from the farm that afternoon. He was on his way back to the Benders where he was needed and where he wanted to stay until his father returned. No-one seemed to be following him and no-one had called over the loudspeaker at the station. "Look out for a young runaway boy, thin, with red hair, goes by the name of Ian McDonald...."

He leaned his head back and thought he might take a nap. Then he realized with a start that his plans didn't include the coming night. It would be very late when he got off at the station and he would be all alone. He didn't know anyone in Kitchener. It would be too late to hitch-hike to Milltown. He couldn't sleep in the railroad station all night; the police would be called to pick him up. He'd read about tramps spending the night in a park. Maybe he'd have to do that. Maybe he could ride to the end of the line on the train and then come back, but the conductor would probably get suspicious.

When the train at last stopped in Kitchener, the two elderly ladies also got off. Someone greeted them and took them to a waiting car. A strange fear settled over Ian. For the first time in his life there was no-one to meet him or take him to some kind of home.

The flashing lights of a hamburger stand down a nearby street attracted his attention and he walked towards it.

"A hamburger and a chocolate malted," he ordered at the counter, feeling better now he was connected with something familiar.

78

"We close in fifteen minutes," a sleepy young waitress yawned. "Your folks going to pick you up here?"

Ian nodded. He wished they were.

He ate quickly. The waitresses clattered dishes and cleaned up the counters for the night. Ian envied them. They would be going home soon. He wrapped half his hamburger in a serviette and hurried to the washroom.

"I'll leave in a minute," he assured the harried staff.

Outside Ian walked slowly down the dark streets. Most of the houses looked cosy with warm lights glowing. What did people do who were homeless? He felt as lonely and deserted as an abandoned house.

He passed a large lawn, recently mowed. The rambling old house in the middle of it looked mountainous in the dark. It must have at least five bedrooms, Ian guessed. What would happen if he walked to the door, rang the bell and asked to stay in one of them? A growl and sharp bark came from the porch. Ian hurried on. In the next block he found an unkempt lawn with yellowed papers thrown about the steps. Surely no-one lived here. No dog barked. Weeds tangled about his legs as he walked towards the house. Then he saw a tent, far back behind a clump of bushes. Could he sleep in it? He walked slowly towards it and listened from the outside for noises. A cricket chirped and that was all.

Carefully he untied the entrance flaps and peered inside. There was a canvas floor and a screen at the door, but the darkness was as dense as layers of tar. Ian swallowed his fear.

"Is anybody here?"

There was no response.

He crawled to the back corner.

"Yiaow ow ow...!" A screech and sudden scratching noise rushed at him. His heart skipped a beat and left him breathless.

"Miaow ..." A small cat rubbed against his legs. Ian gathered it into his arms. The rolled-up Amish pants became their pillow and it was not long before they were both asleep.

Next morning the chugging of a truck woke Ian early. He shivered and reached for a blanket. There was nothing but rough canvas floor. At first he thought he was dreaming. Then he touched the squashed half of hamburger beside him and remembered the night before. The cat was gone, but there was still a warm spot in the crook of his arm and the cold hamburger had been nibbled through the middle.

He walked back to the railroad station, drank some water for breakfast and threw the hamburger into the garbage. He felt sure no-one would be looking for him this early. Maybe Aunt Clem hadn't discovered yet that he was missing. The early morning traffic was confusing. In the daylight, the streets looked even stranger than at night. He was mixed-up about directions too.

A policeman strolled by. Ian wanted to avoid him so he hurried across the street almost bumping into a large, gray truck filled with lumber.

"Watch it!" the truck driver shouted, and then in a more friendly voice asked, "Where 'ya off to, kid?"

"Milltown," Ian answered, trying to sound like it was a trip he made every morning.

"Goin' to see your Grandma?"

"No, my Grandpa," Ian answered, thinking of Jonah.

"Need a ride? I'm goin' out that way." Ian nodded.

The truck bumped along comfortably and Ian was soon asleep. When it stopped, the driver had to shake him awake.

"This is the lumberyard. I'll have to drop you here," he said, opening the high truck door. "You've got about a half mile to go to Milltown."

Ian felt a great need to hurry. The Benders' neighbours couldn't come indefinitely to do the chores. Going back to the farm, of course, meant sore feet and aching muscles. Ian cringed. Why couldn't the Benders borrow a tractor for a couple of days just to get caught up? What if it did compact the earth and produce no manure, as Jonah said. Maybe the farmer across the road would loan them his. He might even have a potato-picking machine. Hours of time could be saved if he and Reuben didn't have to dig and dig and dig. The Benders wouldn't have to own the machines. They could just borrow them for an emergency.

The sleepy village of Milltown appeared. Ian passed a deserted feed store, crumbled and rejected. The only noise came from a café next to the store where the ringing of a pinball machine dinged through the still autumn air. It was nine o'clock and Ian was hungry. He decided to eat something in a hurry and then rush to the farm. He would put on his Amish pants at the end of the Benders' lane.

He walked into the café and found a table at the back near two teenage pinball players who were slouching near the pinball machine. The tall thin one lit a cigarette.

Ian buried his face in the menu folder. When the waitress came, all he could think of was another hamburger and french fries. The pinball players paid no attention to him. One of them, who was short and pudgy, kicked at the machine, calling it a cheat. They returned to their table.

The tall boy, who smoked, stretched his legs over the floor. He almost touched Ian's table with a bare toe that stuck through a hole in his blue running shoe.

"What are we going to do later on?" he yawned, leaning towards his friend. "I've got the car."

"We could drive around; or go to a movie."

"No — too tame. What about that Amish job we never finished? Maybe we should rough them up a little more? None of us have bothered them much all summer."

"Well, I don't know, Pete." The fat boy was hesitant. He seemed nervous and uncomfortable.

Ian was suddenly alert. What did they mean by "rough up the Amish"? The memory of a blue car dragging a smashed buggy, which he had seen from Aunt Clem's car window yesterday, flashed before him. He lifted his head and looked at them.

They were an odd pair to be friends. Pete, the tall one, had a thin sneer and a slouching, bored posture. The other boy was a fat woodchuck, awkward and wary.

Ian must have stared at them rudely for the tall one leered at him and said, "What's the matter, red-head. Want to come along with us?"

Ian was caught off guard. He didn't want anything to do with them.

"I don't know what you're talking about," he answered moving his chair slowly away from their table. Then a new thought jarred him. What if they decided to "rough up" the Benders? His Amish friends had had enough trouble. He couldn't let these two cause any more.

"I don't know what you're planning to do." Ian's voice was shaky, but he continued. "If you're planning any trouble for the Amish, though, I'll report you."

Pete started towards Ian, but the pudgy boy held him back. Pete's light-blue eyes, however, focussed on Ian with contempt.

"I don't take that kind of talk from anybody." Pete's fists clenched and his lips became taut. "You're a stranger here, aren't you? Well I think you'd better leave. You'll be sorry if you don't."

He's a swaggering, bluffing phoney, Ian thought to himself and his temper flared.

"You sound like a cowboy in some cheap film," he said.

Pete was surprised. "I could smash you to pieces — you skinny grade-school smart guy." He was muttering under his breath as the two boys shuffled from their table and walked out the door.

16

Ian was worried. He'd been threatened before by bullies in his Chicago school, but it had never been so personal. Pete could walk right over him; and they had stared into each other's faces. You didn't forget a person after that. It was like taking a fingerprint of somebody's head.

Following directions from the café owner, Ian hurried to the country road leading to the Benders' farm. After about a mile he quickly changed his pants in an empty bus-stop shelter. He had a nagging feeling that the two boys from the café might be following him, but the road was empty. The sun shone and he kicked off his shoes and swung them from his shoulder by the laces. Maybe his threat to tell the police would change Pete's mind about molesting the Amish? He didn't want any more trouble.

Lacy goldenrods brightened the roadside and Ian began to hum a folksong that he and Dad had learned one winter holiday in Switzerland. Maybe he would teach the words to Reuben. The only songs Reuben sang were slow and solemn and in German.

The big white clapboard house, with Jonah's Grossdoddy House hooked onto the side, came into view as Ian turned a corner. The white picket fence around Susie's vegetable garden was freshly painted. There were several horses and buggies tied to posts in the farmyard.

He breathlessly ran up the lane. Mary saw him first and raced to greet him. Sarah toddled close behind.

"Ian is back!" Mary cried.

The little girls grabbed him around the legs and Ian picked up both of them in his arms. Reuben appeared from the barn.

"What's happening?" Ian asked.

83

"Plenty!" Reuben was sober. "But I'm glad you ran away and came back."

Mary interrupted excitedly. "The policeman is here. He says your Aunt Clem got him out of bed at five o'clock. She wants him to catch you and take you back."

"That's right," Reuben added. "Tom Higgins said your father called too. You're supposed to phone him back as soon as you get here. He doesn't care what time of the day or night."

"Well!" Ian dropped the girls to the ground. Why all this swarming and buzzing and acting as if he had committed a crime? He might have known Aunt Clem would get flustered and call the police, even though he'd told her in the note what he planned to do. And why did she have to call his father?

Ian noticed the buggies again. Reuben answered his look.

"Those people are here to help. There's so much to do, Ian, and Momma and Poppa are coming home in a week."

Jonah hobbled down the road and greeted Ian with a hearty handshake. "We're glad to see you, Ian, but you've made a lot of trouble for yourself." He pointed to the police car and then to Tom Higgins who sat grimly behind the steering wheel. Ian noticed Aunt Lydia and Rebecca waving to him from the porch. It was like being welcomed home.

The welcome was brief, however, for Tom Higgins stepped from his car and motioned for Ian to join him.

"You've caused plenty of trouble for me this morning, young fellow." The policeman was gruff. He looked sleepy and irritable. "Now what do you have to say for yourself?"

A singsong rhyme began turning around and around inside Ian's head: "Ask a stupid question, and you get a stupid answer ... ask a stu..." Ian couldn't believe it: he had just come on his own, overnight, all the way from Toronto.

"Nothing," he answered finally. Why couldn't he just get started on some of the work that was needed around the farm? The policeman hovered over him.

"Your aunt is sick with worry. Jumping out of a window in the dark isn't something a twelve-year-old boy does every day of the week, is it?"

"No, sir," Ian agreed. Higgins was being sarcastic and didn't want answers. Adults were like that sometimes. And this policeman just wouldn't stop.

"Your aunt called your father in the Territories.... He doesn't know what to think about you.... He wants you to call him right now, so come with me and we'll stop at the nearest telephone."

For a brief second Ian remembered the two boys at the café and his threat to inform the police. Tom Higgins wouldn't believe a word he'd say right now.

Jonah stood by the car, leaning on his cane. "If you can get your father's permission, we'd like to have you stay, Ian. We can use an extra farm hand."

So Jonah really needed him! Now all he had to do was to convince Dad that he should stay with the Benders. The old man's hand shook as he grasped the top of his cane. His face was pale and gaunt. He stood back with the rest of the family to watch Ian and Tom Higgins drive off.

"He's a good man," Higgins stated as he spun the car back down the farm lane. "This accident will just about finish him."

The accident and the suffering again ... Ian wanted to stuff his ears shut from the sound of it.

The car jolted to a stop before the roadside phone booth. The two of them got out and Ian walked inside.

"Here's the number. You'll need to dial the operator and tell her to make it a collect call."

With a shock he realized that in less than a minute he might be talking with his Dad. He felt shaky inside and wondered if he would remember everything he wanted to say.

"Operator, operator."

A machine-like voice came through the wire.

"A collect call to Andrew McDonald in Inuvik." Ian tried to be calm. "In the Northwest Territories near the Beaufort Sea."

"Do you have the number — the number, please?" the computer-like voice asked. Ian slowly read it out.

"And who is calling, who is calling, please?"

"His son, Ian McDonald."

There was a long silence. Ian held his breath. The wire clicked, then beeped with bouncing bells up and down the scale. There was another long silence.

Finally a voice answered. "Andrew McDonald speaking."

"Dad!" Ian cried.

"Are you all right, Ian? Thank heavens you called! I've been so worried." His father's voice sounded strained.

85

"Of course I'm all right," Ian answered.

"Your Aunt Clem called five hours ago," his father shouted over the crackle of the line. He sounded both angry and relieved. "She's frantic. She said you climbed down a tree and ran away. She thinks you're trying to join the Amish."

"Dad, please," Ian interrupted. "You've got to listen to me." Surprised by his father's outburst, he started at the beginning, just as he had in his letter. Soon it was like having his father in the telephone booth with him. "Yes." "I see." "That's too bad," came from Dad's end of the wire. Ian ended his story then took a deep breath.

"I've got to stay here and help the Benders," he said. "Aunt Clem doesn't need me. You don't have to worry, Dad."

"Well I'm sorry, Ian, but I *am* worried. I feel like coming down there straightaway, but there's a storm and the threat of an airline strike."

Ian waited.

"Don't be too harsh on your Aunt Clem," his father finally said. "Good manners and order are important to her.... As for the Benders, obviously we'll have to arrange compensation. I can't understand Jack Turner being so irresponsible."

"Dad," Ian interrupted again, "please tell me you believe my story."

"Of course I do. But Ian, an Amish farm is not the place for you to live."

"Dad, the Amish live just like our Scottish ancestors did when they came to North America. You said *they* were brave and courageous." Did he hear Dad chuckle? "I like it here, Dad, and I feel fine. We eat fresh vegetables from the garden every meal. We have plenty of milk. I wrote you a long letter about it."

There was a brief silence.

"Is Aunt Clem right that you want to join the Amish?" His Dad's voice sounded strained again.

"I can't join them. I'm too young. You have to be at least sixteen," he said indignantly.

"Well, that's good to know." His father seemed almost amused. When he spoke again he sounded more relaxed, more decisive.

"All right, Ian. I'll call off the police and Aunt Clem until

I can finish this current project and get a flight down. I'll come to the Benders' farm as soon as I can and we'll make a decision then about where you should stay."

"But Dad I have to stay here because of the accident. Don't you understand? I want to see you, but you don't have to come now. You can wait until Christmas."

There was a pause.

"Ian," his father said with some severity. "I have to do what I think is best. You can stay where you are for the moment, but I want you to call and report to Aunt Clem every few days until I get there."

"I'll report to her, Dad. But I don't want to live with her."

There was another pause.

"I miss you, Ian." Dad's voice was calmer.

"I miss you too," Ian answered.

Tom Higgins rapped on the door. "Let me talk with your father before he hangs up." Now what? What was this policeman going to say to his Dad? Ian reluctantly handed over the receiver after saying a quick goodbye, and walked outside.

A little of the tightness inside him seeped away like escaping air from an overblown balloon. Dad missed him, and that was important. But if his father really believed him, why was he coming to check on him? Why did he still have to make a decision about where he should stay?

17

"You're pretty lucky, Ian," Tom Higgins said as he left the booth. "That father of yours is an understanding man." He stretched his broad shoulders, remembering that he was first of all an officer of the law. "Now you make sure you behave yourself while you're here."

"Yes, sir." Ian clipped off the words like a salute.

Lunch was being served on the lawn of the Bender home when they returned. Tom Higgins said a few words to Jonah then drove away. Two long tables stretched over the freshly mowed lawn. The bearded men with Jonah were served first. Rebecca and a friend, dressed in freshly washed dresses with triangle tops and long aprons to match, carried food from the farmhouse kitchen. But there was none of the gaiety of a picnic.

Ian's appetite bounded with one smell of the large steaming bowl of beef boiled with noodles that Rebecca carried. He sat beside Reuben, listening to some boys of his age chattering in Pennsylvania Dutch. He filled his plate with the noodles, coleslaw, fresh tomatoes, pickled red beets, home-made bread and mounds of apple butter.

Jonah stopped for a moment behind him.

"Eat yourself full, Ian. We're glad you can stay with us for a time."

"*Ich bin hongry!*" Ian answered carefully with his mouth full.

Reuben dropped his fork into his plate. "Ian, that's Pennsylvania Dutch!"

"Maybe I'll speak some more before long." Ian was pleased with himself.

Within minutes plates were wiped clean with bread, and slices of pie appeared on the table.

"Apple schnitz or shoo-fly pie?" Rebecca asked and then laughed at Ian's reaction. "The shoo-fly has no flies and no shoes — just molasses, eggs and a few spices." Ian took both kinds.

He was unsettled by a moody silence from Reuben who sat beside him. Lately they had laughed and joked together, even though Reuben was most of the time a serious boy whose interest in horses and farming was endless. Ian was eager to learn from him. But the sharing was one-way only. Reuben had little interest in Ian's "outside" world. He had no doubts at all about being an Amishman for the rest of his life. They strolled away from the others at the table to water and feed the neighbours' animals.

"Dad says I don't have to go back to Toronto," Ian said, hoping to end the gloom.

Reuben seemed limp, like a paper cut-out of his real self. If he heard Ian, he didn't answer.

"We have to sell the farm," he said slowly, his hands hanging loosely beside him.

"Sell the farm!" Ian exclaimed with disbelief. Jonah had told him how members of the Bender family had come here from Bavaria over a hundred and fifty years ago to settle and develop the farm.

"Poppa is very sick." Reuben spoke even more slowly. "Grossdoddy is too old to farm. Rebecca is probably going to leave and get married. I wish you could stay all winter, Ian. I wish John would come home." A tear rolled down his cheek. "The man across the road with the tractor would pay a lot of money for our farm." His words became almost a whisper.

"But he would ruin the land," Ian said, finding that he no longer wanted the Benders to borrow the red tractor to save time.

"It won't happen. Grossdoddy will take a loss and sell only to an Amishman," Reuben answered. His face turned to Ian helplessly. "I wish the accident hadn't happened."

If he worked on the farm all winter and if John came home, might that make the difference, Ian wondered. Could the Benders then keep the farm?

He must find John.

He'd already asked Reuben, who said none of the family knew his whereabouts. Jonah had forbidden John to come home until he sold the car. Then Ian thought about Elam Stoll, whom he could see talking to Jonah near the barn. Elam was near John's age. Might they have been friends?

He thought about this again through the lazy warm afternoon as he helped Reuben with the animals. Reuben worked listlessly, with no joy even in handling the horses.

Late in the afternoon Ian came across Jonah fanning himself under the maple tree.

"Why are the neighbours here today?" Ian asked.

"They are cleaning up and getting ready to cut the oats and corn and then fill the silo," said the old man. "We always help one another, especially when there is sickness and extra work."

Jonah's eyes never faltered as they looked into Ian's, but far inside them was a pain that seemed patiently waiting to be healed. Ian knew that many things made up the hurt — Hannah, John, Ezra, the farm. He also knew that this was not the time to ask about them.

Dusk came early. Everywhere there were signs of a plentiful

89

harvest. Over the fields a damp haze rose from the earth as if responding to the rising of a full, watery moon.

Ian and Reuben walked with Elam's buggy to the end of the lane. The horse had just been purchased at an auction. Her hair was the colour of toast, with no stripes or dots to mar its smoothness.

"She's a racehorse," Reuben said, pointing out to Ian how slim the horse was and how high she held her head. "She stopped winning in the races and the owner put her up for sale. Elam bought her. Her name is Lightning."

The putter of a car engine was heard coming down the road. Elam pulled his horse and buggy to the side. The soft putter changed abruptly to the swishing sound of wind. A rusted blue car raced towards them, churning up puffs of dust in all directions. The car windows were rolled down and a boy in the passenger seat held one hand out the window, flicking ashes from a cigarette. The other hand held a rock. Ian recognized Pete, the lanky bully from the café in Milltown, the one who'd said, "Let's rough up the Amish." Was he going to throw the rock or was he just trying to scare them?

Pete didn't hesitate. He pitched with a full swing, aiming at the horse. The rock zinged from the window, grazing the horse's tail. Ian watched Pete's face and for a quick second Pete looked at him. There was instant recognition and Ian saw Pete scowl. Then the car spun away, down the country road towards the highway. Ian hadn't recognized the driver — it must be another of Pete's friends.

The racehorse swung her head from side to side. Her eyes were wild and fearful. She leaned forward and started to gallop, all four feet seeming to lift off the ground at once. Elam's new courting buggy rattled behind her.

"I'll get my horse and follow," Reuben cried. He ran back to the barn.

Ian saw the horse and buggy career off the road into a newly ploughed field. Elam strained forward, like a jockey riding in a race. Gradually the horse ran slower. Great chunks of mud clung to her feet. The buggy tipped from side to side. Finally the horse shifted to a canter and came to a stop at the far end of the field.

90

Reuben appeared with Jonah in a small, open buggy. They halted when they saw the horse and buggy standing still in the field.

"Don't follow them," Jonah called. "Elam has her under control."

The three of them waited.

Shy, black-haired Elam, with the shaven face of an unmarried Amish man, walked steadily towards them down the road leading his nervous, twitching horse. Both of them dripped with perspiration.

"It will be a long time before I can hitch her to a buggy again," were the only words Elam said.

Ian was amazed. Hadn't any of them seen the boy throw the rock? Surely they knew what had happened?

"I saw the boy who threw the rock in Milltown," Ian blurted out. "I heard him say he wanted to get in his car and come and 'rough up' the Amish."

Jonah, Reuben and Elam didn't speak.

Ian turned to Elam for some kind of rebuke. He could see why Rebecca liked him. He had a kind, sensitive face. His dark eyes, sunk back a little from his cheekbones, gave him an even darker and more solemn look.

Elam glanced sadly at his horse.

"Whatever is supposed to happen will happen," he said.

"I feel that when you get hit you shouldn't hit back ... but I don't know. It isn't easy."

Ian's anger mounted. He agreed it would be wrong to hit back with a stone, but Pete could have killed the horse and caused another buggy accident. He should be reported to the police and punished.

Reuben harnessed Dick to Elam's buggy and disappeared into the night in the direction of the Stoll farm. Ian asked if he could walk with Elam as he led his skittish mare quietly along a country lane. There was a long silence between them. Ian thought about Elam's buggy wheel in the tree and then his solemn acceptance of the rock throwing. Ian couldn't understand these people. They were daring with their animals and stubborn in their beliefs and yet there was this meekness about accepting punishment which jarred every fibre in his body. The silence became almost painful — two people walking together like floating icebergs. Ian plunged in bluntly.

"Were you a friend of John Bender?" he asked.

"He was my best friend," Elam said plainly.

"Do you hear from him? Do you ever see him?"

"I've joined the church now," Elam answered carefully. "I've accepted the Rules. I don't see John."

"But do you know where he lives or where he works?" Surely a best friend would keep in touch, Ian thought.

"He works in the lumberyard outside of Milltown. He lives in Kitchener, I think." Elam looked sideways at Ian and laughed. "You are full of too many questions."

Ian didn't care. The lumberyard must be the same place where the truck driver had stopped this morning. He remembered the name — "Martin's Lumber." He could call John there on the telephone.

18

A warm sun spread over the Bender farm, giving it the peace of a pastoral painting. But under the surface there was turmoil. At breakfast Jonah sounded confident that God would care for his family: they were blessed to be surrounded by loving friends and grateful that Ezra was coming home alive. But Ian heard sorrow in the old man's voice when he talked about selling the farm and finding cheaper land. He said nothing about the accident or the boy who threw the rock.

"What about Pete?" Ian asked.

"We will not press charges." Jonah's answer was firm.

Ian grew impatient. The Benders could at least talk about Pete; they should talk about John, too. Couldn't somebody just say out loud, "If John would come home and help us, the farm might not have to be sold." But no-one mentioned his name.

There was too much silence! Ian raced up the stairs and filled his pockets with jingling coins. He would report to Aunt Clem and then telephone John Bender. He shouted out the bedroom window to Reuben, "I'm going to call Aunt Clem!", then clattered through the house and ran down the lane. He felt uneasy about connecting himself with Aunt Clem and began rehearsing what he would say. When he walked inside the phone booth, he dialed her number slowly.

"Clementine McDonald speaking," she answered at once.

"Hello, Aunt Clem." Ian hurried. "I'm fine and I hope you are too. If there's no air-strike, Dad is coming to see me as soon as his project ends. Goodbye."

"Ian!" Aunt Clem grabbed his ear with her voice. "It was inexcusable what you did — running away in the middle of the night. I was terrified. You were inconsiderate and ill-mannered." She stopped talking and Ian thought he heard a chuckle. "I must admit I didn't know you had the nerve. Now call me again next week." She hung up.

Ian was jolted. Aunt Clem had talked about his nerve.

93

He would think about that later. His next call took all of his attention.

The number of Martin's Lumber was in the yellow pages of the tattered phone directory that dangled from a heavy chain. Ian dialed it carefully. A woman answered and said she would call John Bender.

A puzzled male voice said, "Hello."

There was nothing to do but burst in on him with a full report.

"My name is Ian McDonald and I'm living at Jonah Bender's farm. I'm the hired man."

The puzzlement changed to surprise at the other end of the line.

"Oh?" John queried.

"Did you know there was an accident? Did you know your father had his leg amputated and that your family will have to sell the farm?" Ian stopped to catch his breath.

"Are you trying to play a joke on me?" The question was not asked harshly but hesitantly, as Jonah would have asked it. "You sound like a young boy. I'm not in touch with my family. I don't know anything about them."

"Then I'll tell you." Ian began with a rush of words that evidently convinced John of their truth for his voice soon changed to shock and then dismay.

"I'll have to see you, but I can't come to the farm." John paused. "You say you're calling from the telephone booth at the end of the farm lane? Wait there for me. I'll pick you up in half an hour."

Ian checked his watch.

"Deposit seventy-five more cents if you want to continue this call." The operator clipped off her speech.

Ian didn't have one cent left. The connection was cut. He walked outside and sat on the grass leaning his back against the telephone booth. The autumn sun was a gift of delicious warmth, not the blistering summer heat that dried your tongue. The quiet around him seemed heavy with the abundance of harvest. Even the bees zig-zagged drunkenly from clusters of goldenrod to yellow ragwort to pale blue chicory. The air smelled of spices and ripe apples. Ian's cheeks were freckled and tanned. His hair flamed with colour and he felt strong enough to pitch a sheaf of oats into the high farm wagon. Mrs. Coutts in Chicago wouldn't know him.

He almost resented the approaching hum of an automobile. How could John get here so soon? But the car wasn't John's. It was Pete's blue rusted automobile. Ian's heart pounded. He thought of hiding in the phone booth. Pete was driving alone. The car passed Ian slowly, then it stopped and backed up. Pete leaned from the car window, tapping ashes from a lighted cigarette.

"So, it's the red-head who seems to have joined the Amish," he sneered, his sleepy eyes sharpening into needles.

Ian's temper flamed.

"I saw you throw the rock at that horse. Why did you do it?" Ian's voice reached into high notes. "The horse was just learning to pull the buggy. You could have killed her."

Pete seemed surprised. He opened the door of his car, smashed his cigarette back and forth into an ashtray and stepped out.

Another car appeared on the road and braked to a stop in front of the phone booth. A stocky young man with broad shoulders, who looked like a young version of Jonah, jumped from the car. Ian knew instantly that it was John Bender. He was a fraction shorter than Pete and had Reuben's steady brown eyes.

"What's the matter?" John asked quietly.

"I'm just about to bloody-up this little Amish fellow with the big mouth," the tall boy said.

John stepped between Pete and Ian.

"I don't fight," he said steadily, "but I can wrestle." He began unbuttoning his shirt.

Pete's voice took on a nastier edge. "I don't see this is any affair of yours."

"This boy here is a friend of mine," John said.

Pete stared at John's muscular chest. He shrugged, sauntered sideways, climbed back into his car and started the motor.

Ian was shaking. He would have been no match for Pete in any kind of fight. He looked at John with admiration. Wrestling was something he would have to learn.

95

"You must be Ian." John sounded undisturbed. He shook Ian's hand and shrugged off the whole encounter by saying, "I know that boy. His name's Pete Moss. He's full of the devil. His parents split up a while ago. He lived with his father for a couple of years, but then his father took off out West." John gestured towards his car. "Maybe we could ride around and talk," he offered.

Ian stepped into a small, new cream-coloured Volkswagen, almost like the one that had belonged to Jack Turner. It gleamed like polished silver. John wore stiff, tight blue jeans and a flashing plaid shirt with red and blue stripes. He seemed amused by Ian's traditional Amish clothes. His brown hair was bobbed around his face like an Amishman's, but a small moustache sprouted above his upper lip. Ian knew that the Amish Rules strictly forbade moustaches, even though they demanded untrimmed beards for married men. Aunt Lydia had told him these rules were made a long time ago to oppose fashionable grooming. John wouldn't be accepted by the Bender family looking like this. How could he ask this modern young man to come back to the farm? Maybe he shouldn't try.

They rode for a few miles without speaking. Ian became uncomfortable. At last John said, "I didn't know there was an accident and that Star was killed." His fingers gripped the steering wheel with such pressure that his knuckles turned white. "It's terrible about Poppa's leg. Tell me everything that's happened since, Ian." John was tense and worried.

Ian poured out the story in detail. It was a relief finally to share it with a member of the Bender family. John stopped the car at one point and wiped his eyes. "Poor Poppa." He seemed badly shaken. "He's a good farmer. We worked together."

"Why did you leave the farm, John?" Ian asked bluntly, knowing that they had to talk about it.

John was thoughtful, but there was a flicker of a smile on his mouth like the one Jonah sometimes had. "I guess it all started with my wanting to own a car. Even when I was a young boy, I took Reuben to the dump near the farm on Sunday afternoons and we sat in an old banged-up car and pretended we were driving it."

"Why didn't you just hide your new car?" Ian asked.

"Reuben told me that some of the Amish boys do that until they join the church."

John laughed softly. "I couldn't hide anything from Grossdoddy." He became wistful. "I miss the farm and all my friends.... I'm like a fish out of water when I'm not with the Amish.... I'm not like Hannah. Reuben probably told you about her. She hated wearing plain clothes and she didn't like farm work. She always wanted to live in the city and be a nurse."

"They need you at the farm, John," Ian said with some urgency. "Why don't you come back?"

John seemed to waver like a man on a tight-rope with a balancing pole. On one side of him was his new way of life in the city with the keys to a shining new car jingling in his pocket. On the other side was his horse and buggy, his family and his separate Amish way of life.

John pressed the gas pedal and the new car bounced over the country road.

"You wouldn't understand — you're just a boy, just an 'Outsider'. Sometimes you 'English' think of the Amish way of life as just a quaint, temporary way to live, something to experiment with. But it isn't. It's a total, lifetime commitment."

John paused, a little ashamed of this outburst.

"If I come back, Ian," he said, "I'm old enough to join the church. You are either in the church or on the outside. There's no place in the middle. If I came home now just because I wanted to help Poppa, I might not be a good Amishman." John pressed harder on the gas pedal. "The decision I make is for the rest of my life."

He stopped the car abruptly. They had driven in a full circle around the country roads and were back at the telephone booth. He opened the door for Ian.

"I'm glad you called me, Ian." John was troubled. "I needed to know what was happening at home. Poppa is a good Amishman and I miss him. He needs me — but I don't know ... I just don't know ... I'm not sure it's possible."

Ian opened the door to step outside but John stopped him.

"I must think hard. Don't tell Grossdoddy or Poppa that you talked with me."

Ian closed the door of the shining new car and walked up

the lane towards the farm. What would he do if he were in John's shoes on the tight-rope? He didn't know.

19

A smaller calendar with a picture of two frisky horses on it hung on the wall in the Bender kitchen. Each morning Ian crossed off a day. He wished he could draw a huge circle around the date his Dad was supposed to come. But it was impossible to predict. There was no news on the farm about an airline strike or further storms in the Northwest Territories. There was no news, either, from John. Should Ian make another phone call? Would John answer if he did?

Sometimes Jonah bought a local paper in Milltown and Ian read each line. He unearthed from the tiny print the scores of his favourite baseball team. He found lists of records that had made the Top Ten and names of movies that he hadn't seen. If he had a radio, he could keep in touch with the world. Maybe he should buy one that didn't need plugging in and stuff it under his pillow.

But who could he share it with? The Benders didn't think about the outside world. It took all of their effort to take care of the soil, live simply in their community and practise their religion.

Another thing he couldn't share with anyone was his unease about Pete Moss, who was sure to get even with him somehow. But this morning Ian was at least distracted by the excitement of his job. Reuben had said he could curry Dick alone. The friendly animal nudged him with his muzzle and buried his head in Ian's neck. Glorious warmth and affection bubbled up inside Ian like uncorked soda water. He rubbed his cheek against Dick's strong, smooth back.

In the stall next to his, Gravy Dan and one of the Gingerich brothers were working and talking in low voices.

"It's sad for an old man to leave the farm he's lived on all his life," the Gingerich brother said.

"Jonah is my lifetime friend." Gravy Dan's voice was burdened. "An old man, a crippled man and a young boy can't run a farm even with good women like Lydia and Susie. Jonah won't let his family become a burden to all of us." He sighed. "If John would come home he could run the farm with Reuben and the new boy, Ian."

The sprightly Gingerich brother laughed. "That red-haired boy would make a fine farmer if he could harness his temper."

The need for John grew like a rolling ball of snow. But did the Gingerich brother mean what he just said, that he would make a fine farmer? Ian was elated. He became a little giddy with this surprise compliment. He wanted to sing, or dance, or just celebrate. He gave Dick a squeeze around the neck that made him neigh, then whispered into the horse's ear, "I'll sit on top of you, Dick, and see what it's like to be a farmer riding his own horse!"

He climbed quickly up the side of the stall, grabbed Dick's mane, and threw his left leg over the horse's back. Was Dick really so wide and so tall? Ian felt like he was sitting on top of a camel.

Dick's ears twitched. He had no training for this kind of behaviour. He reared up gently and sent Ian sliding down his back, over his tail — and into a heap at Gravy Dan's feet.

"Well, Ian." The old man was surprised. "There is a time for play and a time for work. The horse knows better than you."

Ian didn't answer. He was too embarrassed. He picked up the curry comb and stroked Dick's side with fierce vigour.

When his Dad came he could discuss this idea of farming with him. He tried to picture his father in his tweed suit striding through the Benders' barn and over the fields. He could see his craggy face and eager eyes questioning every inch of the farm. His Dad was working in the North with a company that was pioneering into the future. Would he like these people who didn't want electricity, didn't want his kind of progress and held onto ideas from the past?

The morning became warm and sticky with flies. Everyone seemed restless. Even the animals were ill at ease.

"Reuben. Ian." Jonah's call shook Ian from his dreaming.

99

"Fill the buckets with oats and feed the pigs." Jonah's voice was cross and tired.

The two boys met and raced up the slope of dirt to the second floor of the immense barn. They were excited to find a fresh pile of hay in the storage area. It was an invitation to forget their worries and their work.

"I can jump into the haystack farther than you," Reuben challenged.

"Let's see." Ian took a run from the far side of the barn. They both landed in the same place and dug themselves out, laughing.

"Let's tie a rope to the rafters and swing into the hay," Reuben cried, already throwing a heavy rope high into the air over a beam and then tying it tight.

Ian grasped the rope in both hands and swung across the barn. It took the breath from his lungs. Then Reuben took his turn on the rope and landed with a high bounce into the haystack.

"Reuben! Ian!" A stern call came from the barn door. The rope swing dangled in the air and the two boys jumped to attention. A strict, scolding Jonah, whom Ian hardly knew, stood in front of them.

"You are old enough to know that we don't play during a working day. Now get those buckets, fill them with oats and come downstairs at once."

"He means it," Reuben whispered as they hurriedly took down the rope.

The boys worked through the morning without saying much, but by noon Jonah greeted them at the kitchen table with his usual good humour.

After lunch there were scores of upturned potatoes to be thrown into baskets. Ian leaned hot and exhausted against a tree.

"Work can cease to be toil when you begin to enjoy it," Jonah assured him. Ian didn't believe him.

But it *was* enjoyable when the community grain binder came that afternoon with three sturdy horses attached to cut the oats. The tall oat stems fell like hundreds of brown dominoes lined in straight rows. The oats were tied into sheaves and Ian with Reuben and two other boys marched through the fields, setting ten sheaves at a time upright into large bundles called "shocks" to dry until threshing time.

"You should see John set up the shocks," Reuben called to Ian. "He does one by himself faster than two of us working together. He's almost as fast as Poppa." His face clouded. "I mean as fast as Poppa used to be."

There were guests for evening supper and Reuben chopped off the heads of two roosters so that Rebecca could start to cook. Ian held his hands over his eyes when the headless birds flopped around in the grass behind the barn with blood dripping from their necks.

"You wouldn't want to eat them with their heads on, would you, Ian?" Reuben joked, carrying the headless birds to Rebecca who doused them into a pail of boiling water to loosen the feathers.

One of the guests was Gravy Dan, whose long white beard rippled up and then down over his fat stomach as he breathed. He sat in the rocking chair by the stove chuckling over the news he was reading in *The Sugarcreek Budget*, the most popular paper among the Old Order Amish and the Old Order Mennonite people in North America. Once a week it arrived in the Bender mail box from Sugarcreek, Ohio, brimming with reports from hundreds of communities criss-crossing the border between the United States and Canada. Each line carried news of weather, crops, visitors, new babies, the sick and the dying.

"Ach!" Gravy Dan exploded, rocking forward until he almost tipped onto his head. "Our Ian has his name in *The Budget!*"

Ian, Reuben, Mary, Aunt Lydia and Rebecca ran to look. In fine print under Milltown, Ontario, Canada it read:

Ian McDonald of Chicago is a guest of several weeks at the Jonah Bender farm. He is helping with the harvest while Ezra recovers in the hospital from an accident. Ezra had to have his leg amputated. He was hurt when his buggy was hit by an automobile.

Ian was pleased. Now everyone would know that he really was working on the farm. He might send the story to Dad and Aunt Clem.

"Listen to this story from Pennsylvania." Gravy Dan clapped his knees and tipped the rocker dangerously forward. This time he shook with laughter as he read:

"It is rather early to have frost in the early morning hours; but not at the place where the man and wife had an argument while getting out of bed. She said she believes there is frost this morning, the husband doesn't think so and stepped out onto the upstairs porch roof to investigate and slid down over the side. The wife was right, they did have a frost."

At supper, as Rebecca carried a steaming bowl of home-canned beef and gravy to the table, the bowl slipped from her hands and fell. The dish broke and the food splattered over the floor.

Rebecca burst into tears as Sarah and Mary helped to clean up. "It's just that I miss Poppa so — and what will it be like when he comes home and he can't walk?"

20

In the early afternoon of the next day, with the sun still warm and golden in the sky, a long white ambulance drove up the Bender lane. The family stood back in silence as two men lifted Ezra onto a stretcher and carried him to the downstairs bedroom.

Susie, a tiny woman with quick steps, appeared by Ezra's side. She searched for her family and ran to Mary and Sarah, gathering them into her arms. She smiled at Reuben, Rebecca and Aunt Lydia and clasped Jonah's hand. The little girls held fast to her skirt and wouldn't leave her. It hadn't been possible for her to come sooner. She'd seen it as her duty to stay beside Ezra.

"I'm glad you are here," she said directly to Ian before walking into the house. Ian liked her straightforward, affectionate manner.

The family gathered in Ezra's bedroom, speaking softly in Pennsylvania Dutch to the pale, thin man in a white hospital gown. Little Sarah crawled onto the bed beside her father and leaned her head against his shoulder. His long brown beard brushed over the small black cap on her head.

Ian was shaken. This gaunt, fragile man on the bed in front of him couldn't possibly be the sturdy farmer he had seen lying in the field after the accident. That Ezra had strong, sunbrowned hands. This man's hands were white and thin and lay limp against the sheet. As Ian looked at them, remorse and guilt weighed more heavily than ever on his mind.

Mary stood beside the bed near her father. "Does your leg hurt, Poppa?" she asked timidly. Her eyes filled with tears.

"It hurts a little," Ezra answered, his head sinking into the pillows, "but God will give me the strength to bear it."

"I made special bean soup for you, Poppa." Rebecca tried to smile.

Reuben moved close to the bed. Ian saw hurt and misery in his eyes. "I picked the baby pig you said I could raise, Poppa.

She acts just like a baby Rascal." He pretended to be cheerful.

Ezra smiled and leaned back with relief and exhaustion. "You are good children. I am home now and I never want to leave again. I will stay here until I die."

He doesn't know the farm is going to be sold, Ian realized.

The others looked at him with love, and held the wrenching news about the sale for another day.

"The doctor said Ezra should stay in the hospital at least two more weeks." Susie spoke quickly, looking with grave concern at her husband and holding her hands wearily against her head.

"The food didn't taste good. It was too English." Ezra shook his head. "The city air was full of smoke and I couldn't breathe right. I missed all of you and the farm." He leaned back contentedly on the pillows again.

It wasn't until evening worship, which was held around Ezra's bed, that Ian noticed a heavy, thick book called *Martyrs' Mirror* on a nearby table beside the Bible. Jonah pulled the book from the table and holding it in his lap began leafing through it. There were pages and pages of stories about Christian martyrs who suffered and died for their beliefs. Here and there were frightening etchings of men and women being hung on crosses or burned at a stake. Many were Mennonites who lived in the 1500s.

Jonah attempted to explain. "Our people were trying to reform the state church, but the government said they were destroying it."

Ian was repelled. How could people do this to one another? Why did the Benders want to keep such a book in their home?

"What does all this have to do with the Amish?" he wanted to know.

"Yah, Ian, I already told you some of the story of our people." Jonah leafed through the pages of the big book. "In here is our whole history and stories and pictures of the persecutions."

The girls had fallen asleep on their father's big wide bed. Ezra ran his fingers over Sarah's soft cheek. He lay back on his pillows, tired and pale, though his cheeks were red and feverish.

"The story of our people prepares us to suffer," he said quietly. "We are tested by it."

104

Were Pete and his fellow vandals supposed to be part of this suffering, Ian wondered.

There was a long silence. No-one spoke even when they lighted their kerosene lamps and went upstairs to their bedrooms.

21

"Will the harvest ever end?" Ian burst out after a day of apple picking.

"You'll be glad for all of the food when you're hungry in the winter," Jonah reminded him.

And, as if to speed things up, a playful frost came at night and threatened to shrivel the tomato vines.

"We must pick them at once or they will freeze." Susie and Aunt Lydia scurried about with their long skirts flapping. The events of the last few weeks were temporarily forgotten in the

rush of the harvest. Ian and Reuben were needed in the garden to rescue every cucumber, squash and tomato; and they were needed in the barn, too, where old Prince, who now had double work because of Star's death, was ailing. A veterinarian was called and giant pills had to be stuffed down the animal's throat.

On such a bustling work day, a letter arrived for Ian from his Dad. "Inuvik, N.W.T." was printed inside the round postage mark. The entire family gathered around Ian on the porch as he spread out the pages in front of him and began to read aloud:

"I wish you were here with me, Ian — though it's dreadfully cold. I'm helping to build an oil rig on a man-made island in the Beaufort Sea. The closest settlement is Inuvik, Canada's northernmost incorporated town."

The Bender family listened with puzzled faces. Ian read on:

"Under the ice in the sea are millions of barrels of oil. It's the world's last frontier. I'm troubled each day about the effects of this drilling and of possible oil spills. How much are we injuring the lives of seals, polar bears, and the native people?"

Soon Ian stopped reading aloud. The letter was becoming personal. The others drifted away. Ian gathered the pages together and sat on the porch steps alone to finish it.

Dad wrote about the Benders' kindness and said he would repay them.... Jack Turner had disappeared.... And then, at the end of the letter, the words stood bold and threatening in front of him.

An Amish farm is not the place for you to live, so I've enrolled you in a Toronto Boarding School for boys. I'll take you there when I arrive....

The airline strike had been averted and his father was coming in three weeks! The letter ended:

Remember, Ian, the above is a compromise. Since you don't want to live with Aunt Clem, I've given you another choice.

Ian felt hollow, as if somebody had knocked all the air out of him. Dad hadn't really listened to him on the telephone or tried to understand his letter. What kind of compromise was his father offering him? He didn't like the alternative any better.

"You look sick, Ian," Ezra said with concern, leaning forward in his wheelchair. "Do you want to go upstairs and lie down?"

"Yes," Ian said and listlessly climbed the stairs. He lay flat on his back on the bed and stared out the window. Dread of entering another new school in another new place and all alone spread through him like an illness. His head ached. The worries about Pete and about John crumbled away into little pieces. He probably would never see either of them again.

An hour passed and pans began to rattle in the kitchen below Ian's bedroom. The smell of frying chicken wafted through the open air vent on the floor. Aunt Lydia called for him to come and eat. He brushed his hair quickly around his face and walked slowly down the stairs. It would be three weeks until Dad's visit. He would try to forget the letter, pretend it hadn't come. When he thought about three weeks, the days started to stretch before him like a year.

Ian joined the Benders at the table, but when Rebecca brought his plate of crisp, fried chicken, he wasn't hungry. Ezra sat near him in his wheelchair, ashen and shaking.

"Grossdoddy has just told Poppa about selling the farm," Reuben whispered to Ian.

Ezra's eyes blurred. He dabbed at them with the sleeve of his shirt, then searched the faces of those around him. He looked puzzled and confused as if begging for someone to help him understand. The weak, sickly man he had become seemed a stranger to him. He rubbed his thin white fingers over the blanket that covered the stump of one leg and the virtually useless limb of the other. He had lost his legs. Now he was going to lose his farm.

"Has God deserted me?" he cried out with terrible anguish. He wheeled himself from the table and went to his room. No-one spoke and no-one followed him. Ian was shaken. Little Sarah whimpered and ran to her mother. Jonah bowed his head.

At sunset, when the sky glowed with streamers of crimson and gold, Ezra appeared on the porch.

107

"Will you take me on a trip around the farm," he asked Reuben and Ian.

They pushed him in the wheelchair to the yard. Mary and Sarah ran beside them. Susie called with a worried frown, cautioning them to be careful. Aunt Lydia came out to tuck a blanket securely around Ezra. Rebecca chased flies from her father's face and hands.

As they walked slowly without speaking, Ian felt a momentary peace in spite of his feelings of guilt about the accident and his frustration at having to leave the farm. The orderly farmyard with the straight furrowed fields, the weeded garden, the white picket fence, the still blooming marigolds, the plentiful harvest were all in tune with the beauty of the sunset. But Ezra's eyes were turned inward and he felt only the loss of this peace and beauty.

"I think we could keep the farm if you would stay, Ian, and if John would come home," he said so softly that only Ian, who stood closest to him, could hear.

That night after Reuben and Ian were in bed, Ian tossed about restlessly.

"Calm down, Ian," Reuben confronted him. "I might as well be sleeping with a colt."

"Sorry." Ian turned towards the wall. He desperately wanted to talk with Reuben. They were friends now. But would it do any good? Ian's departure would just make Reuben more miserable. It might even speed up the sale of the farm. But if John —

That's it! He would tell Reuben about John. He'd only promised not to talk about him with Ezra and Jonah.

"Reuben."

"Now what?" Reuben answered sleepily.

"I've seen John," Ian whispered.

"John!" Reuben popped up in the bed like a jack-in-the-box.

In a hushed voice Ian confided the whole story, even John's request that he keep the meeting a secret.

"I'm glad you saw him," Reuben whispered. "I want him to come home."

They talked eagerly. What could they do to convince John?

"I'll call him again tomorrow." Ian promised. "I'll tell him about Ezra at supper tonight."

How did John look, Reuben wanted to know. Ian didn't mention the moustache. He described the car and told Reuben how John said he felt like a fish out of water when he wasn't with the Amish.

The clock downstairs struck midnight before the boys finally slept. By mid-morning the next day, Ian and Reuben had finished the chores in record time and suggested to Jonah that they check on the mail in the box at the end of the lane. Ian mentioned innocently that he might also call Aunt Clem and get his regular report to her off his mind.

"Remember, Reuben, the telephone is only for emergencies. You stay outside the booth when Ian calls." Jonah was speaking in his Bishop's voice.

There was no mail, so the boys went at once to the phone booth. Ian propped a stone against the door to hold it open so Reuben could listen without coming inside. A chilling wind spun crackling leaves around them.

Ian dialed the lumberyard number. The bell rang and a woman's crisp voice answered instantly.

Ian spoke quickly. "I need to talk to John Bender. It's very important. Could you call him to the phone?"

There was a long wait.

"I'm sorry to take so long," the woman apologized. "John Bender doesn't work here any more. Someone says they think he's taken a new job in Toronto. Anyhow he didn't leave a forwarding address. I wish I could help you." She hung up.

"Did you hear, Reuben?"

"Yes," Reuben said quietly. "He's not coming home."

They walked dejectedly back to the farm, kicking at the fallen leaves around them.

"I'm not giving up yet." Ian tried to sound hopeful. But he had to admit John might well have decided not to be an Amishman for the rest of his life. John had every right to decide this, he supposed, but he felt somewhat sad and betrayed.

22

Early Monday morning Aunt Lydia walked down the road ahead of Mary, Reuben and Ian with books tucked under her arm. It was Ian's first day of Amish school and Aunt Lydia was the teacher. Her scholars — as Ian soon discovered the Amish call their students — greeted her along the way. "Hello Lydia." Titles were never used.

Before the four of them had left the farmhouse, Susie had packed their lunch pails and Ian had noticed "John" scratched on the bottom of his. It was almost as though he were taking John's place.

The warmth of Indian summer persisted and everyone walked without shoes on the sandy dirt road. Blackbirds whistled in the yellow maple branches and Mary picked a lacy spray of goldenrod for Lydia's desk.

A red-brick schoolhouse with a bell on top appeared behind a row of tall green pine trees. For a long time, Lydia told Ian, it had served all the farm families in the area until the yellow school buses came and took many of the country children to new consolidated schools in the towns and villages. The Amish would not go, for the new schools had television sets, radios and movies and demanded that shorts be worn in the gymnasium.

"If our children learn too much about the world, they might fall in love with it," Jonah had warned the parents. So the Amish financed their own schools and paid the public school levy as well. The government authorities were tolerant.

Lydia walked inside the school building to pull the rope that rang the ancient school bell. As it tolled through the still morning air, a car buzzed noisily at the far end of the road. When it cruised closer, Ian's stomach sickened. The car was rusty blue and Pete Moss was at the wheel. His fat friend sat beside him and another teenage boy leaned forward from the back seat.

The Amish children ran from the road into the field, alarmed

110

by its speed. Ian lingered behind. He could at least pretend he wasn't afraid. The car slowed down beside him.

"So *this* is the school the red-head goes to," Pete called out. His friends laughed.

Ian bristled. "That's right. This is my school. Do you want to make something out of it?"

"Don't get fresh with me, kid. You don't want your friends to get hurt, do you?" Pete glared at Ian, who could feel his heart thumping in his throat, but was determined not to show his fear. He walked towards the car and shouted,

"If you hurt any of the Amish I really will report you to Policeman Higgins!"

"He'd never listen to a runt like you," Pete sneered. "Any more threats from you and I'll burn down one of their barns."

The car sped away.

A chill shot down Ian's back. He ran through the field to be with the other boys and girls.

"We get off the road for cars like that," Reuben cautioned. "Grossdoddy says they're the work of the devil."

Ian agreed. But the Amish way of dealing with "the devil" was to ignore him, whereas he seemed to clash head on!

Inside the school, it was safe and serene. Straw hats and black bonnets were hung on the hooks in the cloakroom and lunch boxes were lined up in the corner. Eight rows of desks faced the teacher. Grade eight, which had the biggest chairs, was where Ian and Reuben sat. Grades one and two had the smallest chairs. Mary dangled her bare feet in the air from one of them. Long before the day was over, she fell asleep.

Roll was called and a chapter was read from the German Bible. A German prayer was said and a hymn was sung in unison. Then the language for the school day changed to English.

Grade two printed numbers on the board. The upper grades stood and recited multiplication tables in a chorus. Grade eight was assigned a reading lesson from *Our Heritage*. After they had finished, Ian, Reuben, Amanda Zehr and a girl named Johanna were called up to the recitation desk in front of the room. Lydia asked difficult questions about what they had just read.

Ian listened to the younger children recite and found himself fascinated by their pronunciation lesson. He repeated the multiplication tables with Grade five over and over. Maybe he would finally learn them and also come to terms with the metric system.

Eventually it was recess. A surge of boys and girls broke into the quiet autumn and teams were chosen for baseball. Lydia swung the bat to open the game. The ball zinged far into the field. Ian was proud of her. The players ran fast and hit the balls hard and the smallest children chased them into the distant fields. Lydia rang the school bell and everyone gulped water at the pump before going inside.

It was a beautiful school, Ian thought, but he could only go to it for two weeks. He looked at the newly ploughed corn fields from the open windows and at the red geraniums in tin cans blooming on the window sills. Lydia had drawn a flower box on the board. Each of them would pick a favourite flower and put its name into the box.

When lunchtime came there were liverwurst sandwiches on

thick slices of home-made bread. Ian had never tasted anything so good. And when the school day ended, all the desks were tidied, the floor was swept, the blackboards washed and the erasers clapped together until they were clean. There was a moment of silence.

"Goodnight, Lydia," the boys and girls called out as they put on their black bonnets and straw hats, left the schoolroom and skipped down the road.

The next day it rained, but the children plodded smiling under big umbrellas to their red-brick cross-roads school. Lydia walked ahead as always. They were near the entrance when all of them stopped. Bricks had been thrown through the windows and many of the panes were broken. The vandalism was ugly and without meaning, like a slap on the face of a very small child. The boys and girls could not go near because they were barefoot.

"Wait in the shed under the pine trees," Lydia called to them.

Ian shuddered. There was no doubt in his mind that this was Pete Moss' doing. So this was how he was getting even with him. It was like war. Pete was willing to attack whole communities just to punish one enemy.

Whatever I do, Ian thought, I seem to bring trouble to the Amish.

Lydia sent for help from the nearest farm. Horses and buggies arrived with men who carried hammers and saws. The window frames were scraped and cleaned and boarded up.

"Tomorrow we will put new windows on the side of the school that doesn't face the road," one bearded man said. "The windows can't be broken as easily from there."

No-one asked who caused the wreckage, and on-one was angry but Ian.

That night in the Bender kitchen Ian pleaded with Jonah.

"It's wrong to break windows," he argued. "Pete and his gang are dangerous cowards. They should be locked up in a jail."

Jonah's answer came with great sadness. "We are like Abraham in the Old Testament," he said. "When his enemies shut up his wells, he dug new ones. When our enemies break

113

our windows, we replace them. If we fight them, Ian, we become like them."

How could he argue with Jonah? But it could only inflame Pete and his gang when the Amish didn't seem to react or want revenge.

When Ian entered the school house the next morning with the other boys and girls, new windows lined the opposite side. It was as though the building had been turned around to shut itself off from the road and the cruel rocks and meaningless taunts of Pete and his bullies.

23

Ian was beginning to feel as plagued upon as the one-room school house. All his plans had struck dead ends, and he and Reuben had given up hope that John would come home.

It was painful each day to watch Ezra withdraw from his family. He seldom talked. His skin stretched white and transparent over blue throbbing veins. He hardly touched his food.

"I'm afraid he's slowly killing himself," Susie said despairingly.

At every meal there was talk about selling the farm. Prospective buyers came to inspect the house and barn, but each time the family held back, postponing a decision.

Ian worked each day with Reuben until his muscles ached. By now he was becoming quite good at the jobs Jonah assigned him. What would the family do when Dad took him away? The volunteer helpers among the Amish couldn't keep coming day after day.

Then one evening there was a surprise. A telegram was brought to the door for Ian. He and Reuben were in the barn when Mary called loudly for him to come to the kitchen. The Bender family stood around the lamp as Ian ripped open the yellow envelope. He read aloud:

"GOT EARLIER FLIGHT. WILL ARRIVE FOR CANADIAN
THANKSGIVING. LOVE, DAD"

"That's in just two days," Susie exclaimed. "We'll cook a
special Thanksgiving dinner just for Ian's father."

Dad's coming was not going to be a time of celebration, Ian
wanted to tell Susie. But he hadn't felt able to talk about his
departure. The rumpled letter that told about the boarding
school was still in his jacket pocket.

The day before Thanksgiving at the school, the boys and
girls sang slowly and in English, "Come ye thankful people
come, praise the song of Harvest Home." The day after
Thanksgiving would be Lydia's birthday and the scholars
were planning a party for her. Amanda Zehr had invited the
whole school to her farm for lunch. A pain knotted in Ian's
stomach; he would not be there for the party.

The thought of leaving the farm for a strange school was
unbearable. But he was still excited about his father's coming.

He hadn't seen Dad for a full month. Would they know each
other? He remembered his father's long hurried steps when he
walked.

"When my Dad walks," he told Reuben that night, "he
gallops like Elam's horse the day he got hit by the rock."

"This will be the first time I ever met a man who looks like a
horse," Reuben chuckled.

Ian threw a pillow at his head.

Early on Thanksgiving morning, Reuben and Ian feverishly
cleaned every inch of the barn in preparation for Andrew
McDonald's visit. Ian was restless all through the morning's
work and by lunchtime was fretting that bad weather might
have grounded his Dad's plane. Late in the afternoon, though,
they were in the corn field hitching Dick to the hand-plough
when a strong, low-pitched voice cried "Ian!"

Ian turned around and there in the farmyard was his Dad. He
ran into his arms and they held each other tightly. Some of the
anger and hurt against his father began to drain from his heart.
Dad stood him away at arm's length. Astonishment and admiration surfaced in his kind, rugged face.

"I can't believe the change," he said. "In one month you

115

have grown, you look stronger and healthier. The Benders have performed a miracle." But he also winced as he realized what Ian was wearing.

"Do you have to wear those Amish clothes, Ian?"

Ian looked at his father's smartly tailored tweed suit and his necktie that matched his shirt. Were these old-fashioned clothes one of the reasons Dad wouldn't let him stay? He began to be concerned about the visit. Quickly, however, the excitement of Dad's presence restored his good humour. He broke away and pulled his father towards the corn field.

"Watch how I can plough a straight furrow!"

Reuben yielded the wooden plough handles to Ian. Ian gripped them and set his eyes on the white rag that flapped far away on the opposite fence.

"Giddyup," he called to Dick and walked steadily ahead. He finished one furrow, turned around and came back through another.

"It's the straightest one you've done, Ian," commented Jonah, who had come up to join them and stood leaning on his cane beside Ian's father.

Ian felt very proud as he introduced them. Then he took Dad's hand and led him to the barn, where they were joined by Mary and little Sarah. Ian picked up Sarah and carried her. Mary hung on to his suspenders.

"Sarah can't speak English yet, Dad," Ian said. "She speaks Pennsylvania Dutch."

"Are you learning it too?" Dad asked in a constrained sort of way. Ian nodded.

The four of them walked into the lower floor of the big bank barn and strolled from stall to stall. The collie followed behind them barking. Ian and the little girls called each animal by name. It was hard for Ian to remember that he had once been afraid to walk behind Bessie or to touch Dick with his huge metal horseshoes.

Lydia rang a bell for dinner and the family — and Andrew — all washed together at the outside pump.

"Lydia is my teacher at the school," Ian confided in his father with a note of pride in his voice.

"And how is school?" Dad asked.

"I like it," Ian answered at once. "It's more fun than it was in Chicago."

116

They walked past the outside toilet on their way to the kitchen. Dad looked disapproving.

"Jonah says you have to deny yourself earthly comforts," Ian explained.

Andrew McDonald frowned. "I don't mind the idea, Ian, but in some places those things are a health problem."

Dinner was a grand occasion. Every member of the family shook Dad's hand. Ezra wheeled himself to the table and sat at one end beside Andrew. There was an awkward moment until he suddenly said bluntly, "I'm trying to forgive the man who ran into our buggy, Andrew. I think I could do it if he would come to see me."

Andrew McDonald seemed uncomfortable. "I'm deeply sorry about the accident, Mr. Bender. It's a strange thing about Jack Turner. He quit his job and no-one knows where he's gone."

"Then I think he's running from a guilty conscience," Ezra said quietly.

Ian couldn't relax. Though the conversation was mostly about farming, any minute now Dad might mention the boarding school. But the subject didn't arise. The silence after the meal seemed shorter than usual. Jonah brought it to a close by producing his atlas and opening it to a map of the Arctic Circle.

"It's a holiday." He was almost jovial. "Let's take some time off from the work and hear about this North country."

Andrew McDonald stretched himself comfortably and spread his large hands over the table. He liked to tell about his travels. Ian wondered what his father was thinking about the bare walls, the curtainless windows and the floors without rugs. He admired his father's ability to jump from one country to another and from century to century with his long strides and quick interests and be at home wherever he went. But Ian was uneasy. Dad could be interesting and polite with all kinds of people, but it didn't always mean he approved of them.

Andrew McDonald leaned over the kitchen table, which had now been cleared of all food and dishes, and ran a bony finger over the map. He came to the winding Mackenzie River where it flowed into an ice-blue Beaufort Sea and began by talking about life in Inuvik.

The Benders, even tiny Sarah who couldn't understand

117

English, were captivated by this unusual man, who with a map and with the sweep of his words lifted all of them from the warmth of an Indian-summer day in Ontario to early winter snow storms and the eternal permafrost of the Arctic. His word-pictures held them entranced.

"I spent one night with an Inuit family on the snow," Ian's father said, drawing all of them further into the biting Arctic cold. "They were making camp beside a herd of cariboo. The way they set up their deer-skin tent and anchored it to the ground with snow was magical." He began pushing make-believe snow across the kitchen table and pounding it down over make-believe stakes.

"The wind howled and beat against the hide, but inside we were warm and comfortable with a stove and a pipe the Inuit family had brought with them on their sled." Dad rubbed his hands together in front of a make-believe heater. Mary shivered.

"The cariboo are the Inuit's shelter and food." Andrew McDonald frowned. "But the drilling of oil may destroy these animals as well as the Inuit way of life which has been in existence for centuries."

The whole family nodded. They wanted to hear more, but the chores could not be postponed any longer and Ezra had fallen asleep with one hand over the stump of his aching leg.

Ian twisted about nervously in his chair. Dad hasn't mentioned the boarding school because he thinks I've already told the Benders, he thought to himself. Other thoughts drummed in his head: I've got to see Dad alone and explain that I can't leave the farm so soon.... I could start the boarding school after Christmas and still keep my part of the compromise.

Jonah interrupted with plans of his own.

"You must come to my part of the house, Andrew," he directed. "I think we have something to talk about. You want to preserve the land God created in the North. I try to preserve the land God gave me to take care of right here."

Andrew McDonald smiled and followed the old man from the table. Reuben left for the barn. Ian wanted to interrupt, since there wasn't much time to try to change Dad's mind, but they would need to be alone. He followed the two men into the Grossdoddy House. Ian had never been inside it before. The rooms were small and barren, but so clean that he hesitated to put his dirty bare feet onto the polished linoleum.

If Dad tells Jonah about the boarding school now, I'll just have to argue in front of both of them, he thought. He jumped inwardly with each tick of the noisy clock above Jonah's small stove. Andrew McDonald settled himself into a rocking chair. He was relaxed and at ease and not at all hurried. Were the two men just going to visit all evening?

Jonah smiled, then bent forward tensely from his straight-backed kitchen chair. His white beard jutted forward over his dark blue home-made shirt like an exclamation point.

"Much of the farm land around us is being destroyed by large-scale operators," he said. "They take over more and more land to make money with cash crops. When you farm this way year after year, the top soil runs off into the Conestoga River and disappears."

Jonah could be as dramatic as Dad, Ian thought. "Large-scale operators" began to loom in his mind as gangsters.

Dad bent forward in his chair too.

"What are your people doing about this, Jonah? Many of us think your way of life is old-fashioned and backward."

"Yah, well," Jonah said pensively, "we have small farms, maybe a hundred acres. We work hard and keep all our family busy and well fed. We rotate the crops and spread manure over our fields. Ezra, J—" he paused, "Reuben and I plant fruit trees, soybeans, all kinds of grain, corn and clover. Susie, Rebecca and Lydia raise vegetables and melons. It seems to me we produce better food than a hundred-acre unit which yields nothing but cattle feed and beef, or nothing but hog feed and bacon."

Jonah smiled at both Ian and his father. "Your Ian is a good worker, Andrew. We couldn't get along on the farm without him."

Ian gasped. Jonah was counting on him to be a regular farm-hand. He started to speak, but Jonah didn't stop.

"And about being backward, Andrew" — he became thoughtful — "we Amish believe that we aren't here to have a good time, or to make a lot of money or become famous. We try to do the will of God, love our fellow men and prepare for eternity."

119

Dad closed his eyes as though trying to shut out a painful thought.

"I was a farm boy once," he said, half opening his eyes and focusing them far out the window into the night. "My father was a stern man and a hard worker. He had rigid rules that were enforced with the strap. He believed that God was always on his side. I couldn't take his harsh discipline and the endless work, so I ran away when I was sixteen and I never went back."

Ian stared at his father. Grandfather McDonald had been dead for years. This was the first time he'd heard Dad talk like this about him.

"Yah, well," Jonah nodded with sympathy. "We Amish are also guilty of too strict discipline sometimes. A boy or a girl is like a horse. Make them work too hard and punish them too much and they'll balk."

Ian thought of John and of Hannah.

Jonah turned to look at Ian. "I think Ian wants to be a farmer."

Ian was startled. He had intended to tell Dad about this himself. And after what his father had just said about farming, Dad would surely talk now about leaving for the boarding school.

Instead Andrew McDonald stretched out his long legs. He took up almost all the space in Jonah's little room. He was quite relaxed. Maybe he hadn't heard what Jonah just said.

"Every single thing you Amish do seems to be based on your religious beliefs," Andrew said slowly. He looked with interest at Jonah and kicked off his shoes. "I couldn't live under all your severe rules, Jonah, and I prefer to put my beliefs to the test in the world. But obviously you Amish should have the right to practise your religion the way you think best as long as you're not doing any harm to others." He cupped his chin in his hand. "It's rather like allowing the Inuit to keep their way of life in the North. They're preserving important values and a sound environment, and I guess you're doing the same thing here."

He stopped talking for a moment and looked curiously at Ian.

"I've never heard you say you wanted to be a farmer, Ian —

120

though I can just see all those old McDonald ancestors wagging their heads in support."

It was getting late and Ian was tired.

"Time for you to go to bed," his father said and got up to walk outside with him.

"We can leave in the morning, Ian." Dad seemed thoughtful. "I wouldn't mind talking a little more with Jonah, then I want to take you to school in Toronto myself and get you settled."

Ian took a deep breath to steady himself. He had expected this, but he felt shaky. He knew now he couldn't just walk away from the farm, leaving them to the dangers and threats of Pete and his gang, and he had to make at least one more attempt to find John. A new idea was becoming clear to him: even if the Benders didn't know it, they were more and more counting on him to take John's place.

"Dad, I've got to talk to you before we can leave."

Andrew McDonald raised his eyebrows in surprise.

"What's this? You aren't planning to run away again, Ian?"

"Of course not," Ian said impatiently. "This is much more important."

"All right," his father agreed. "We can drive into Milltown and have breakfast together tomorrow morning before we say goodbye to the Benders."

He squeezed Ian's shoulder affectionately and turned back into Jonah's Grossdoddy House.

Watching his father, Ian felt his stomach sink right into the ground. What could he do? Tomorrow might be his last day on the farm.

24

Ian plodded slowly up the stairs to the boys' bedroom. Reuben was sprawled over the bed sleeping soundly. Ian shook him awake.

"I'm leaving in the morning," he blurted out. "Dad is taking me to a school in Toronto."

Reuben was dazed. "What did you say, Ian?"

121

Ian repeated his announcement. Reuben shook his head and rubbed his eyes.

"I thought you liked it here, Ian."

Ian didn't answer.

Reuben protested. "I want you to stay. You aren't an 'Outsider' any more ... we're friends, Ian. We can ice-skate in the winter together. Prince will pull our sleds to the top of the hill behind the barn.... I can't do all the chores without you."

Ian crawled into the wide farm bed.

"Couldn't you run away again and come back to the farm?" asked Reuben.

"No, it's different this time." Ian stumbled for words. How could he explain Dad's compromise? "I'm going to try to change Dad's mind in the morning, but I don't think I can," he said.

They continued to talk, stopping only once when they thought they heard a car engine sputter in the field. As they finally settled down to sleep, however, they heard muffled noises coming from the animals in the barn. Both boys listened. It grew quiet. But an odd smell was seeping through their open window. It had a singed odour like burning toast. Outside the window some pigeons circled strangely in the dark sky. The boys climbed out of bed to watch them.

Smoke was curling upward in surging billows from one end of the barn and leaping yellow flames were starting to crackle through it like banners flapping frantically in the wind.

"The barn is on fire!" both boys yelled. They could hear the collie barking wildly in the farmyard. They dressed quickly and ran down the stairs into the kitchen. Susie, Lydia, Rebecca and Jonah were there grabbing their coats from the wall hooks and pulling on rubber boots. Jonah seemed stunned. Susie shook him and pointed outside where the flames were growing in intensity.

"God help us," he cried hoarsely. He quieted himself and began giving orders. Andrew McDonald entered the room with his hair uncombed and shirt unbuttoned. Ezra appeared in his wheelchair.

"Push me outside so I can see," he demanded. Susie ran to his side to obey.

"Reuben and Ian, go to the barn at once — but be careful."

122

Jonah's voice was calmer now. "If it's still safe, lead the pigs out to the garden and take care of the horses.... Susie and Rebecca, unhitch the cows and free the chickens.... Andrew, run to the phone box and call the fire truck.... Lydia, watch the house and the two girls."

Ian and Reuben ran into the safe end of the barn and raced through to the horse stalls. Dick and Prince were prancing wildly.

"I'll handle them," Reuben cried. "You take care of the pigs, Ian. Open the gate to the pig pen. Shove Rascal out the side door to the garden. The others will follow. They won't run away if they can root for potatoes and carrots."

Smoke billowed through the far stalls. Ian held his hands over his mouth to hold back the choking fumes. The three fat sows squealed and shoved inside their pen. A burning timber blocked the entrance, searing the animals each time they touched it. Their squeals had the sound of an ambulance siren. Ian banged the timber aside determinedly with a stick and flung open the gate. Rascal barged ahead, lumbering through the barn at such speed Ian could hardly keep up with her. She sniffed fresh air and food and broke into the garden with the other sows and baby pigs grunting and nudging behind her. Her snout ploughed into the vegetables that were still in the ground. Above the pigs, chickens squawked and clucked and flew in all directions.

Ian started back towards the barn and saw Reuben shoving Dick towards the open door. The big horse was shaking and twitching his head from side to side nervously. A smoking beam plunged from the roof at the far end. With a thunderous crash it landed on the pig pens where Ian had been a minute or two earlier. Sparks sprayed over the barn floor. Dick jumped back, pushing Reuben deep into some hay, then he charged towards the flames and the security of his stall.

"Ian, Reuben, where are you?" a low, steady voice called.

"We're here, Dad," Ian cried out, "near the horse stalls." As he spoke, he yanked Reuben from the hay.

Andrew McDonald ran towards the horse. He carried a large blanket in his hands and seemed to know at once what to do. He threw the blanket over Dick's head, covering the horse's terrified eyes from the spitting fire. Dick quietened gradually and Dad nudged him gently towards the door. Ian lost sight of his father, as Andrew led the horse into the yard, but he could hear his voice calling loudly:

"Come outside now, you two. It's not safe in there. The fire truck is on the way."

"We still have to save Prince," said Reuben. The two boys turned to his stall.

Then Ian heard another voice coming from the farmhouse. It was Mary crying, "No Poppa, come back, come back!"

Ian was puzzled. "Ezra wouldn't come into the barn, would he?"

Reuben looked worried. "Poppa would think about the animals and the barn before himself."

Reuben swung a blanket from a hook on the wall to cover Prince and began to lead him to safety. Suddenly the lapping, unchecked flames burst into a new spray of sparks. They had found the haystack on the second floor and in hideous glee sent puffs of flame and smoke twisting upward. As Ian ran towards the door, he saw a man stretched out on the floor. It was Ezra! His wheelchair had tipped over out of reach and he was clutching for it with his fingers. He really had pushed himself into the barn when Mary cried out to him.

Ezra's outstretched hand suddenly fell back motionless. Ian dived for the limp hand and yanked it with all his strength, pulling the crippled man through the thick smoke. Ezra began coughing and struggling for breath.

"Come on!" Ian gasped. "It's not much farther."

The molten heat burned his throat. He sucked in short, quick mouthfuls of air and kept his head as low as possible near the freshest air. Then he saw the garden and lunged for it like a circus tiger jumping through a fiery hoop. The cool, fresh air was like a sheet of ice-water hitting his face.

Ian and Ezra sprawled over the soft, moist earth. Ezra's fragile hands were scratched and bleeding and his one pathetic leg lay awkwardly over a clump of rotten cabbage leaves. Ian hadn't the strength to lift him.

"You saved my life, Ian." Ezra laboured for breath. "I haven't been forgiving about the accident. I haven't been willing to accept it." There was relief in Ezra's voice, as though a battle inside him had finally been settled. "The bitterness is gone, Ian." He continued to struggle for breath. "God must still have some purpose for me. You've helped."

Reuben ran towards them, pushing the blackened wheel-chair. He lifted his father into it and then looked anxiously at him and at Ian.

"Are you both all right?"

Ian's eyes stung from the heat and smoke, but he hadn't been burned. He looked at the dishevelled man in the wheelchair. It seemed Ezra had forgiven him for the accident. He couldn't explain it, but he too felt enormous relief.

As Ian lay on the ground to regain his strength, he noticed a pile of cigarette stubs in the grass nearby and in the middle of them a leather key ring with the initials R. S. cut into the side.

"That doesn't belong to any of us." Reuben was puzzled.

So was Ian. Then a tingling fear sent chills down his back. He remembered the threat Pete Moss had made that morning near the school — 'I'll burn down one of their barns.' But the initials R. S. had nothing to do with Pete. Ian slipped the key ring into his pocket.

A clanging fire engine appeared, its red paint glittering in the yellow blaze from the barn. Prince and Dick reared into the air from their hitching posts. The pigs lifted their muddy snouts and grunted. The collie began to run around in a frenzy. Buggies, wagons, cars and more people arrived. The crowds strained with impatience until a stream of water finally sprayed over the fire through a long hose attached to the trough near the windmill.

Ian sat in the water-soaked garden too exhausted to move. He watched the hoses being lifted by the fireman and then levelled towards the barn. The powerful sprays cut through the flames and smoke. It was like a war between fire and water, he thought, grateful that so much help had come.

Finally the water began to gain control. It slowly snuffed out the anger of the flames and cooled the smouldering timbers. It dampened the smoke into low puffing mushroom clouds. The stinging tongues of fire flickered hopelessly, then fell like feathers into the sloshing mud.

A contingent of buggies swished through the crowds, riding easily over the damp, sticky earth that cars and onlookers had to avoid. An army of suspendered, blue-shirted Amishmen in black rubber boots surrounded Jonah and his family. The black-bonnetted women had already entered the farmhouse with bowls and baskets of food.

"Lead the horses to the shed," Ian heard a Gingerich brother call. "Fence in the pigs." He could see Elam swinging his arms and his father helping with the animals. Gravy Dan also appeared, to place a consoling arm around his best friend, Jonah. They were silent with each other for so long Ian thought they must be praying.

Susie and Lydia came over to Ian and shook his hand with gratitude.

"If you hadn't pulled Ezra out of the flames, he would have burned to death." Susie's eyes filled with tears. "I don't know what possessed him. God bless you for this, Ian."

But Ian's mind was not on Ezra at the moment. He was thinking about Pete. If Pete had set the barn on fire, that was a serious crime. He could be put in jail for arson. Ian pictured him like a cornered fox in a Milltown jail cell. Then he remembered what John had said about Pete's father abandoning him to go out West. Ian knew his Dad would never just leave him, and for the first time began to admit that maybe his father had had no choice about going North without him. But now he had

found another place he could live for the next six months....
Why wouldn't his father trust his decision?

By this time the Amish neighbours had found temporary
shelter for the rest of the bewildered farm animals. They began
to jog home wearily in their buggies, scraping over the roads
on steel-rimmed wheels. The fire engine rolled away silently
on its rubber tires. It was a surprisingly warm night. A gentle
light from the full harvest moon fell over all of them and
seemed to blot out the ugly wound on the ground from the
ruthlessness of the fire.

Andrew McDonald came over to Ian, reached for his hand
and drew him away from the others. The Benders disappeared
into the farm kitchen.

"Their family needs to be alone," Dad said.

"Our family needs to be alone, too," Ian answered soberly.

"You've been a great help to the Benders. I don't know how
you did it." Andrew McDonald viewed his son with calm
satisfaction. "And you were very brave tonight. I was proud
of you."

The turmoil and worry that had been building up for weeks
inside Ian suddenly surfaced.

"But I haven't really helped the Benders, Dad!" he burst out.
"If I hadn't been in the car with Jack Turner, Ezra would still
have both his legs and the Benders wouldn't be selling the
farm!" Tears began to well up in his eyes. "And if I hadn't met
Pete Moss, the barn might still be standing. He threatened me
and I talked back to him."

Ian wiped his face with his father's handkerchief that was
held out to him. He was surprised at himself. He hadn't cried
aloud like this since he was eleven and his pet cat Mitzie had
died.

"What do you mean the barn might still be standing if you
hadn't met Pete Moss?" his father asked sharply.

"It's a long story, Dad." Ian's words still came in broken
sobs. "I'll tell you in a minute."

"All right, Ian." Andrew McDonald looked at his son with
grave concern. "But let's talk about this for a moment —
because it sounds to me as if you're blaming yourself for things
you didn't intend to do." He paused to be certain Ian was
listening. "You didn't want the accident to happen. You didn't

127

want Ezra disabled. You didn't want the barn to burn. You're not in the least bit responsible for all this suffering."

Dad's words came like a cool salve being rubbed on a festering sore. Some of the guilt that had been weighing him down started to dissolve and wash away. But there were still problems. Lots of them.

"Now, Ian, tell me about this Pete Moss," his father said urgently.

Ian's voice quivered, but he told his father everything — about the café, the rock, the threatened beating, the broken windows at the school, and finally about Pete's threat to burn down an Amish barn.

Andrew McDonald fingered the key ring with the initials R. S. on it.

"This could be very serious," he said. "There may be something for us to do here.... Look, I'm going to cancel my flight tomorrow and stay two more days. I think I'll go into Milltown tonight, stay there and take this key ring into the police station in the morning. But don't mention this to anyone on the farm." He clasped Ian's hand. "I really am proud of you, you know."

Ian smiled. "Does that mean I can stay on the farm — that I don't have to go to Toronto?"

His father was thrown by this change of direction. His chin jutted forward stubbornly. "Now look, I thought about the boarding school very carefully before I came, Ian, and I made up my mind. The Amish way of life is too foreign for us."

"Foreign!" Ian exploded. "What do you think your way of life is on those dangerous man-made islands in the Arctic Ocean! You even stayed in a tent in the snow and got there by dog-sled. How familiar is that?"

He hadn't been so angry since he left Chicago. Dad was still going to force him to leave.

"There's no point in our losing our tempers, Ian." Andrew McDonald walked slowly to a dry pile of fallen leaves and sat down in them. Ian waited a moment and then joined him. His father waved his long fingers over the ploughed fields and harvested garden, which lay bathed in moonlight.

"What makes you think you want to be a farmer, Ian?" he said quietly.

"That's easy to answer, Dad," Ian said, relieved at the switch of subject. "I like taking care of the animals. I like walking behind the plough and keeping the furrows straight. Jonah says I'm getting better.... And I'm like you, Dad, I want to look after the environment. Why can't I stay here for the next six months? I don't want to go to another school. I'm needed here ... I'm doing some of John's work."

Andrew McDonald laughed. "You don't give up, do you, Ian?" He was thoughtful. "You can't take John's place. Don't you see the pressures that would put on you? But I'll think about it, Ian. Give me another day. Now you better get some sleep. Help Reuben with the work in the morning and tell the Benders that I had to change my plane tickets. I'll come and pick you up sometime in the morning."

Ian ran for the open door of the farmhouse kitchen. He wanted to tell Reuben that Dad might change his mind. At the door he turned to look at the smouldering gap where the barn had stood. The farm had been crippled just like Ezra.

25

A heavy silence fell over the Bender farm the morning after the fire. Like soaked cotton it suffocated those beneath it. No words could ease the loss of the beloved barn.

Neighbours came to sweep away the debris and scrape the ugly soot from the crevices of the barn's foundation walls. The walls stood in the bright morning sunlight like pale, empty, outstretched hands. Ezra wheeled himself around with purpose and determination in his dark brown, red-rimmed eyes. No-one talked about the fire. Everyone was too busy.

Ian become increasingly worried about his Dad. He constantly watched the lane and listened for the sound of his rented car. As he watched, Mary and little Sarah crept quietly beside him and reached for his hands.

"You pulled Poppa out of the fire," said Mary. Ian walked with them to the swing under the maple tree where Elam's buggy wheel had dangled in the upper branches. He was lifting Sarah into the swing when Dad's car whizzed up the drive.

Andrew McDonald threw a package into Ian's arms from the open window.

"We have to go into town to the police station," he called. "I bought you new pants and a shirt, Ian. Put them on and we'll drive over."

Ian's temper flared. He wanted to throw the package back and make up his own mind what he wanted to wear. Then he thought about it: if he was going to see the police it might be best not to pretend he was an Amishman. He gave Sarah a push in the swing and raced away to the boys' room.

The clothes felt awkward and tight, but they did fit. The colour was green which Dad claimed went best with his red hair. He couldn't tell because there wasn't a mirror in the room.

He joined his Dad who was outside with Jonah, Ezra and Gravy Dan. They seemed surprised by Ian's clothes.

"I sometimes forget you are an 'Outsider'," Jonah said.

They all walked over to the smouldering foundation of the once-great barn, Andrew McDonald pushing Ezra's wheelchair.

"The foundation is not so bad." Gravy Dan kicked at the newly-swept cement and it didn't crumble. "We must have the barn-building before the snow."

Ian and his father were puzzled. What barn-building? Snow might come as early as November. Was the old man dreaming?

"You mean a year from now?" Andrew offered.

Jonah turned to Ian and his father and said, "We build new barns together. A hundred and forty Amishmen will come to help. A new barn goes up in one day."

Andrew laughed. "I happen to be an engineer, Jonah. That doesn't sound possible."

"Then you should stay and see."

"We'd better explain, Jonah," said Gravy Dan. "It takes two weeks to get ready. First we find an old barn and tear it down. Then we mark each piece and haul it here by wagon. We make the old foundation solid too."

"There's the old Zook barn that needs to be torn down," said Ezra. The three men forgot about Andrew and Ian as they discussed their plans.

As soon as there was a pause in the conversation, Andrew

said carefully, "Well, Jonah, it's time for Ian and me to go into Milltown. The police will be waiting for us. They have proof that a boy called Pete Moss and a friend of his, Roland Stubbs, were near the barn last night before the fire started."

"*That's* what the R. S. stood for on the key ring," Ian exclaimed.

Dad went on. "They are fairly sure Pete Moss started the fire. Both boys were arrested this morning, but the father of the Stubbs boy posted bail to keep them out of jail. There will probably be a trial."

Ezra and Jonah were silent. Theft or murder could be dealt with by Amish prayers. But senseless destruction was another matter.

"That boy Pete is lazy and filled with the devil," Jonah finally said. Ezra added: "When a boy has no work he gets into trouble."

But Ian found this forgiving approach annoyed him.

"Pete can't just run loose till he gets some work," he argued. "Surely he ought to be punished."

Andrew McDonald interrupted. "You saw some of the evidence last night, Ezra, when Ian pulled you out of the barn. The police want you to testify, but Jonah told me about your Amish beliefs on courts and trials, so I told him I didn't think you would."

"That's right." Ezra's steady brown eyes looked directly into Andrew's.

Andrew continued. "Ian, you and I are going to talk with Pete and Roland at the police station." He turned to Ezra and Jonah. "Do you want to come along?"

They shook their heads.

Ian and his Dad sped away over the country road. Ian rolled down the window to feel the speed of the wind in his face. He was nervous about this meeting with Pete and Roland.

"What happened, Dad, when you gave the key ring to the police?"

"They already suspected the boys," Dad answered. "The fat boy, Roland, who is only sixteen and three years younger than Pete, broke down and told his parents about the fire when he got home last night. He claimed he had nothing to do with starting it and threw all the blame on Pete. He also told them about the other incidents with the Amish that you described to me. His parents were horrified. They know Tom Higgins and called him at once last night."

Ian was surprised. He'd never thought much about the fat boy, whose name he'd never heard before.

"When I gave the police the key ring they lost no time in arresting Pete and Roland. That's when Mr. Stubbs posted bail for them."

They reached the outskirts of the town.

"I've already talked with the police and Roland's parents," Dad explained. "I think you need to tell those boys why you are living with the Amish and how generous and kind they have been to you. Maybe you also want to say something about the earlier incidents."

They parked the car on the main street and walked inside the small station. An officer took them through to a small room where Policeman Higgins and a third officer were sitting with Pete, Roland and a middle-aged couple whom Ian took to be Roland's parents.

Pete was slouching in a chair directly in front of Ian. He would not lift his head, but just stared at the floor.

Then Ian saw Roland, with blotches of red over his round face and swollen, tearful eyes that he wiped with a wad of Kleenex. His father, a portly man, sat beside him in an immaculate gray suit with the tip of a gold pen gleaming from its pocket. The frail woman on the other side of Roland sat with her hand on Roland's knee.

"I suppose she loves him," Ian thought with a sting of jealousy.

Tom Higgins introduced Andrew McDonald, who quickly turned to Ian.

"I'd like my son to tell you why he's living in Milltown with the Amish family whose barn was burned to the ground last night."

Ian spoke quietly — was the Amish way having an influence on him? He described the accident, Ezra's operation and the weeks he had spent with the Benders. He told about Elam's horse and the school-house windows. Every now and then Roland sniffed into his Kleenex. Then Ian talked about the fire. Pete didn't move or lift his head.

"Why did you do it, Pete?" Ian looked at the motionless boy.

The policemen raised their eyebrows and Dad stepped in quickly. "This is not a trial. It is not an interrogation. No-one has to speak." He waited. The room was silent.

Then Andrew McDonald began to speak. "I've always believed," he said, "that when people break just laws in a society, they must expect to be punished. If we allow people to throw rocks at an Amish school and burn an Amish barn, their next step may be to throw rocks at a public school, a bank, a lumber company, or a private house."

Andrew sighed deeply. "Ian told you how the Amish gave him a home and love and care at a really lonely time in his life." Andrew smiled. "I could never become an Amishman. But these people have some of their own laws too. They try to live separate from the world and meet its evils by 'turning the other cheek'. This is the way they understand the Bible." Ian's father paused again and surveyed the tensely quiet room. Everyone seemed to be listening except Pete who appeared to have turned to stone. "A good government will always allow citizens to practise their religious beliefs so long as they don't harm anyone else."

Andrew then leaned forward and looked at Pete and Roland.

"Ezra Bender, who has just had a leg amputated, who may lose his farm, and who has now had his barn burned down, will not testify in court against either of you. He does not want you to go to prison. He thinks he should love you as his enemies.... I couldn't do this, but I defend his right to believe it."

Pete looked up suddenly, obviously surprised by what he had just heard.

"And one last thing," Andrew added. "The Amish, with their simple farming ways, are doing a great deal to save our precious environment. Shouldn't we all leave them in peace?"

Andrew McDonald decided not to invite discussion. He explained that he had to set out for Toronto, shook hands with Mr. Higgins and the other men in uniform, took Ian's hand, and they walked from the room. Outside they jumped into the rented car and sped down the highway towards the Bender farm.

"That must have seemed rather hurried, Ian," Dad said. "But I think we had to do it that way."

133

There was silence between them. Since Ian agreed with everything his Dad had said, he wondered whether he ought now to accept his father's compromise.

After a while he said quietly, "I'll be ready to go to the boarding school whenever you say, Dad."

"Boarding school?" said his father, and paused. "Well ... well, I think maybe we can forget that. Because if you want to be a farmer, Ian, you'll have to stay with the Benders until spring and learn to be a good one. And Ian, I want you to report to me on that barn-building. If the Amish can do it in one day I'll have to come and study engineering with them."

Andrew McDonald became more serious. "I'm pretty certain that Pete and his friend will no longer bother you or the Amish. You're too young to be a witness at their trial, Ian, but I don't think those two will forget what you said today."

Ian was speechless. But his Dad couldn't stop talking.

"I'll be leaving for Toronto as soon as I've dropped you at the farm. There are some things I have to settle tomorrow with Aunt Clem. We'll see each other at Christmas.... And by the way, Ian, it looks like I'll have to stay on in Inuvik next summer. But I won't be out on the rigs. Would you like to come up for the summer?"

"Do you really mean that?" Ian's eyes were shining. So were his Dad's.

26

"Five o'clock. Time to get up. Barn-raising day," Susie called softly through the open door of the boys' room.

Reuben and Ian flew from their bed. Chores must be finished and breakfast eaten quickly, for when the clock chimed eight, a hundred and forty Amishmen, with scattered Mennonite and Lutheran neighbours, were due to appear. Some of them would arrive in heavy horse-drawn farm wagons loaded with lumber and tools. Others would ride in their own buggies armed with hammers, crowbars, chisels, ropes, sturdy pike poles and an adze.

No time would be wasted from dawn until dusk. A master

carpenter had been chosen and would call out orders; each man would know his job.

"Poppa was the master carpenter once," Reuben told Ian sadly. "Today Elam will do the job. John was learning it too."

John! Ian had almost forgotten about him.

"Why are you going to do so much work if you are selling the farm?" Ian asked Jonah and Ezra.

"Who would want a farm without a barn?" they answered simply.

It was now six weeks since Andrew McDonald had driven from the Bender farm in the late afternoon with the cuffs of his tweed coat singed and the collar of his striped shirt smudged with soot. He had left when the great bank barn was nothing but a heap of ashes, scattered tools and broken timbers. He wouldn't recognize the scene today. Not one misplaced stick from the ruins of the fire could be seen and the repaired foundation walls were ready for a new bank barn.

"A whole new barn can't go up in just one day!" Ian was still incredulous.

"Wait and see." Reuben smiled shyly.

Ian had not had a free minute since his father left. There was school and the party at Amanda Zehr's farm. One of the birthday gifts for Lydia that day had been a live, fat hen that squawked about the school-room until Lydia herself scooped up the bird in her arms and stuffed her into a box. Reuben had hovered around Amanda with blushes and giggles until Ian was embarrassed for him.

The old Zook barn five miles down the road had been torn down piece by piece to be used for the new barn. The sturdy timbers had been lifted with ropes, but not before the wooden pegs had been pounded out and tenons carefully marked.

Ezra had supervised the work from his wheelchair and called out, "The frame must fit together like a jigsaw puzzle when we take the pieces to our farm."

The criminal pranks of Pete Moss and his friend Roland Stubbs had leaked through the village of Milltown and beyond. A newspaper story had appeared and been copied and printed in other papers. People stopped by to look at the burned foundation of the once-fine barn. Some brought cameras and began snapping pictures.

135

"It will be good when they all go away again," Jonah complained. "I don't enjoy living in a museum or a zoo, or whatever you would call it."

Some people in Milltown felt the boys should go to jail. Others disagreed. "Maybe they didn't mean to start the fire. Don't be too severe on them. Boys have played pranks on the Amish for many years."

Roland Stubbs' parents, shocked at their son's involvement, guaranteed that Roland would work in his father's lumberyard for the next three years if he were spared a prison term, and that part of his salary would go to the Benders to pay for the barn.

Pete's father apparently couldn't be found and Pete remained sullen.

"He started the fire deliberately," most people said. Ian believed it too. But he couldn't stop thinking about Pete's father running away and the effect this might have had.

The trial was coming soon and the sentences would be announced then. The Amish community was silent on the matter, but Ian thought about the trial constantly.

Ezra, who was growing stronger now, was again asked to testify.

"No," he answered with the same certainty. "I get angry sometimes when I think about those boys, but I don't want to be against anyone. It isn't the right way to live."

At seven o'clock the workers began to arrive for the barn-raising. Ian saw Rebecca smile when Elam lingered near the porch. Her dark eyes stole frequent glances at him.

"It's supposed to be a secret that they'll get married," Reuben laughed to Ian.

"Everybody knows, don't they?" Ian shot back.

"But you don't *say* it...." Reuben sometimes grew impatient with Ian's questions. "First the wedding date is announced in church. *Then* everybody can talk about them."

Rebecca, Susie and Aunt Lydia scurried barefoot with pots, pans and food from the kitchen to the emptied chicken house. The place was as clean as a restaurant, Ian noticed, sticking his head through the door into the long shed that now housed tables, benches and a cooking stove.

Twenty Amish women appeared to help the Benders

136

prepare the plentiful mid-day dinner for the volunteer barn builders.

"Let's see." Susie rhymed off the totals. "Ninety pounds of beef, eighty pounds of potatoes, five gallons of apple sauce, pies, cakes, salads...."

Ian was already hungry just listening to her.

Mary and Sarah were shunted to the shaded grass under the apple tree for the day. They had their dolls, a swing and a jumping rope.

"No children can come to barn raisings," Mary told Ian. "It's too dangerous. Timbers could fall and hammers could drop through the air."

"We can only carry tools and nails," said Reuben. "We have to be fourteen to help with the building."

When the two boys saw Elam swing his square in the air and shout for the men to gather on the new barn floor which had been laid the day before, they hurried to the site.

"Carry in the timber, assemble the first bend," Elam called. A hundred hammers pounded in the wooden pegs.

"All together," Elam cried again. "Gather around the bend." The men lined up around the bend, a large section of the barn frame that would support the rafters of the roof.

"Ready? Yo heave! Yo heave!"

Some men strained to pull the ropes, others pushed with pike poles which they had speared into the base of the heavy timbers. They struggled and pushed until the heavy frame moved from the floor. The props had been put in place and the bend was now four feet above the floor. The men paused to rest their backs.

Ian and Reuben watched from the side. They held their breath with wonder that men could push and pull such a heavy load. Jonah and Ezra conferred with one another and gave suggestions to Elam.

"Yo heave! Get your pike poles! Yo heave! Heavy on the rope! Yo heave!"

Then it was time to lift the second bend, then the third, fourth and fifth. Ian and Reuben watched intently all through the morning.

Finally, "Time for dinner!" Elam's call rang above the pounding hammers. Washtubs were strung along the yard for

137

cleaning up. The men were ravenous as they entered the scrubbed and delicious-smelling chicken house. There was room for only half of them to eat at one time. Reuben and Ian waited for the second shift.

"After dinner the rafters will go up, Ian," Reuben said excitedly." The man who climbs to the centre at the top has to be very brave. Some day I will do it."

"Some day I will too," Ian said, shading his eyes and looking far up where the highest rafter would be placed. His heart jumped to his throat at the thought of climbing so high.

As he squinted into the sun, he noticed that the men on second shift waiting near the washtubs were pointing towards the road.

Is something wrong, he wondered.

A hoarse cry nearby shifted his attention to Jonah, who also motioned to the road.

"It's John!" Jonah's voice shook. He picked up his cane and hobbled towards the lane. Ezra swung his wheelchair around and followed close behind. Reuben and Ian ran to join them.

It *was* John and he was leading a sleek brown horse!

Ian could see that he was pale and thin. But his hair was the right length. It was bobbed all around like that of the other young Amish men. His moustache was gone and he wore his baggy, home-made Amish clothes. Ian wanted to welcome him with a loud "Hurrah". This was what he had hoped against hope might happen. But he kept quiet, knowing that no welcomes are ever shouted by the Amish.

Hammers stopped pounding on the new barn. Women and men crowded at the open door of the chicken house. Sarah and Mary ran from the apple tree calling their brother's name.

As John drew near, he reached for Jonah's outstretched hand and grabbed his father's shoulder with his other hand.

"I've come home," he said simply, "and I want to stay." He glanced joyfully around the farmyard at his family and Amish friends. "I've thought hard and long about it. Being an Amishman is the kind of life I was brought up for."

He looked directly at Jonah who stood bent and silent as tears fell down his cheeks and into the soft folds of his beard.

"If the church will forgive me, I'm ready to join, Grossdoddy."

138

He turned to Ezra. "I sold the car, Poppa, and bought this hackney from the race track. His name is Tim. He can take Star's place."

Susie, Aunt Lydia and Rebecca hurried down the lane to stand by Ezra's side. Susie placed a reassuring hand on her son's arm. The collie ran with wagging tail to John's side and licked his hand.

"Did you know about the fire and the barn raising?" she asked.

"The stories were in the newspapers. I read it everywhere." John smiled warmly at her.

Then John waved to Ian. "It took me a long time to make up my mind, Ian. Then I had to find just the right horse."

The Benders — all except Reuben — were astonished. How did John know their young visitor? Reuben, however, welcomed his brother with a wide grin and stroked the head of the new horse, Tim.

"Take care of him for me, Reuben," John said. "I think I'm needed at the barn."

He walked quickly to join the other men.

By the middle of the afternoon the rafters were up and the roof was sheathed with metal. At the very top was John, swinging his hammer from the centre of the highest rafter: he seemed to be holding the whole structure together. There was a rhythm to his movements which Ian doubted he would ever

be able to match. The older men like Jonah, Gravy Dan, and even Ezra from his wheelchair, hammered at the siding near the ground. By evening the barn was closed in.

A few weeks later Ian sat alone under the kerosene lantern at the kitchen table. The others had gone to bed. He smoothed out a large piece of paper and addressed an envelope to Andrew McDonald, Inuvik, Northwest Territories.

Dear Dad:
    I'm looking out the kitchen window at the new bank barn. It still seems like a miracle. You will have to take that building lesson from the Amish when you come for Christmas.
    The trial of Pete and Roland was held last week. The Benders didn't go, so I didn't either. But I read about it in the paper. Jonah, as Bishop, wrote a letter to the judge, saying that the boys have already suffered for their wrongdoing and it wouldn't do any good to send them to prison.
    When the sentence came, Roland was given a one-year term and Pete three years. But the judge suspended their sentences and put them on probation for the same number of years. They have to work and pay part of their salary to the Benders.
    The strange thing about Pete is that he decided to do some work for the Benders instead. But only for Ezra, who takes him around the county to help tear down old barns. Ezra says he's a slow worker, but is getting better. He also says that Pete is another burden the Lord has asked him to bear. But he says this with a twinkle in his eyes.
    I know now that I'll always come and visit the Benders. And maybe I really will become a farmer some day. I'll see how the winter goes. I'm looking forward to the Arctic next spring.

Love,
Ian

Ian sealed the letter and then walked to the window to look again at the new barn. It glowed in the moonlight, its old timbers breathing with new life and new usefulness.

It was years and years ago, it seemed to Ian, that he had lived in Chicago and built a shelter for the white rat Angel with his friend Tony. Tony would split his lungs yelling if he could see all the space on the Bender farm.

"Now I have Reuben for my friend." Ian began talking to himself as he sometimes did late at night when he was alone. "And I won't lose him even if I move away."

He felt happy and free of burdens. John had come home to help save the farm and had brought a new horse for Reuben to take care of. Ian could see how much happier and relaxed the whole family seemed.

He thought about Pete, his first real enemy, and the way this mean, sullen boy had now attached himself to Ezra. He was beginning to believe that the Bible verses the Amish tried to practise about "turning the other cheek" and "loving your enemies" might even work. Indeed it might be the only way to change an enemy into a friend.

It was getting late and the lamp began to flicker, for the kerosene was almost gone. Ian ran his fingers through his rumpled red hair and pounded his fist ever so lightly on the window sill. "I'm going to learn everything about being a farmer before I leave for Inuvik in the spring," he said to himself.

He looked fondly at the plain, scrubbed, old-fashioned kitchen.

"This is one of the best places I've ever lived," he thought — and then smiled. "And I chose it myself."

NOTE TO THE READER

In the United States and Canada the Old Order Amish people are easily confused with the Old Order Mennonites because they both drive horses and buggies instead of cars, they both wear plain clothes and they are both descendants of the radical reformers of the Protestant Reformation in Switzerland in 1525.

At first these reformers were known as Anabaptists because they opposed infant baptism. Later they were called Mennonites after a Dutch leader, Menno Simons. The Amish broke away from them in 1693 and followed a leader named Jacob Ammann. They migrated from Europe to Pennsylvania in 1737 and to Ontario in 1824. There were later migrations of Amish from the United States to Ontario in the 1900s. The Amish worship in their homes, the married men wear beards and the women wear only solid colours. The Amish far outnumber the Old Order Mennonites in North America.

The Old Order Mennonites left the main group of Mennonites in North America in 1893. They worship in meeting houses, their men are clean-shaven and their women wear printed cloth garments.

Notes

Page 46. Jonah's statement about lawyers and lawsuits is taken from *Amish Society* by John Hostetler, Johns Hopkins University Press, 3rd. ed. 1980, p. 252.

Page 53. The verse "Along the line of smoky hills ..." was copied from the blackboard in a one-room Amish schoolhouse in Ontario. No name attached.

Page 92. Elam's statement about not hitting back is a quotation taken from "Killing of Amish Child in Indiana Strains Relations Between Sect, Neighbours," an article in the *Kitchener-Waterloo Record*, 26 March, 1980.

Page 102. The story about frost in the morning is taken from *The Sugarcreek Budget*, Sugarcreek, Ohio, September, 1975.

Page 119. Jonah's statement about producing better food on his farm is taken from *Mennonite Country*, text by A.K. Herrfort, Sand Hills Books, Inc., St. Jacobs, Ontario, 1978. His statement about not being here to have a good time, but to do the will of God is taken from "Beyond Bonnets and Buggies," in *Family Life*, Pathway Publishers, Aylmer, Ontario, May, 1980, p. 7.

Page 136. Jonah's comment about living in a museum or a zoo is taken from *Amish Society* by John Hostetler, Johns Hopkins University Press, 1980, p. 310.

Page 137. The barn-raising instructions ("Yo heave!...") are taken from *Separate and Peculiar*, by Isaac R. Horst, R.R. 2, Mt. Forest, Ontario, p. 42.

Bibliography

DEANGELA, MARGUERITE, *Yonie Wondernose*, Doubleday, N.Y., 1944

FLINT, JOANNE, *The Mennonite Canadians*, Van Nostrand Reinhold Ltd., Toronto, 1980

FRETZ, J. WINFIELD, *The Mennonites of Ontario*, Mennonite Historical Society of Ontario, Waterloo, Ont., 1974

GINGERICH, ORLAND, *The Amish of Ontario*, Conrad Press, Waterloo, Ont., 1972

GOOD, MERLE and PHYLLIS, *20 Most Asked Questions About the Amish and Mennonites*, Good Books, Lancaster, Pa., 1979

HOSTETLER, JOHN A., *Amish Society*, 3rd ed., Johns Hopkins University Press, 1980

HOSTETLER, JOHN A., *Amish Life*, Herald Press, Scottdale, Pa., 1981

HORST, ISAAC R., *Separate & Peculiar*, published by the author, Route 2, Mt. Forest, Ont., 1979

HERRFORT, A.K., Mennonite Country, Sand Hills Books, Inc., St. Jacobs, Ont., 1978

LUTHY, DAVID; STOLL, ELMO (eds. and authors); STOLL, JOSEPH (ed.), *Our Heritage, Seeking True Values, Step by Step, Thinking of Others*, Pathway Reading Series, Pathway Publishers, Aylmer, Ont., 1968

LUTHY, DAVID; MILLER, ELIZABETH; STOLL, ELMO (eds. and authors), *Living Together*, Pathway Reading Series, Pathway Publishers, Aylmer, Ont., 1978

MEYER, CAROLYN, *Amish People—Plain Living in a Complex World*, Atheneum, N.Y., 1976

NAYLOR, PHYLLIS R., *An Amish Family*, Lamplight Pub., Inc., N.Y., 1977

SMUCKER, DONOVAN E., *The Sociology of Canadian Amish, Hutterites, and Mennonites, a bibliography*, Wilfrid Laurier University Press, Waterloo, Ont., 1977

YODER, JOSEPH W., *Rosanna of the Amish*, Herald Press, Scottdale, Pa., 1973

ZIELINSKI, JOHN W., *The Amish — A Pioneer Heritage*, Wallace-Homestead Book Co., Des Moines, Iowa, 1975

OTHER PUBLICATIONS

Sugarcreek Budget, The, Sugarcreek, Ohio — weekly newspaper.

Family Life, a monthly periodical, Pathway Publishing Corporation, Aylmer, Ontario